A Diamond in the Rough

Dr. Cassundra White-Elliott

This book is a work of fiction and was created from the author's imagination. Any resemblance to actual events is merely coincidental.

Published by CLF PUBLISHING, LLC. 3281 E. Guasti Road, Seventh Floor, Ontario, CA 91761. (760) 669-8149.

Cover Design by Senir Design. Contact information- info@senirdesign.com.

ISBN # 978-0-9892358-9-1

Printed in the United States of America.

Dedications

This book is dedicated to all my readers. Enjoy the reading, and enjoy the ride.

Special thanks to the model on the cover: Lashanea Winfield- thanks for doing an awesome job of posing for the cover.

Chapter One

On a Sunday afternoon, Kyra sat drinking tea in a local Starbucks, while occasionally lifting her eyes from the newspaper to watch the couples stroll up and down the street. They all looked happy, but she felt a wave of loneliness fill her stomach.

After finishing her Danish and tea, Kyra decided to do some shopping at the mall next door. As she surveyed the stores, choosing only a few garments to add to her already extensive wardrobe, she came across a newly remodeled health spa. She decided to go in to see if there were any vacancies in the next couple of hours. After the receptionist informed her of the available times, Kyra convinced herself to have a make over. "Maybe this will help in the romance department," she whispered to herself.

"Well, maybe I can help you out there," a voice said. Kyra was so startled, she dropped one of her packages. She hadn't intended for anyone to hear her. "No, thank you," Kyra replied as she turned to see a man with a gorgeous caramel complexion and strong muscular arms that Kyra could imagine circling her petite body. The look in his eyes dismissed her thought that he was using a line on her.

"Well, if you change your mind and would like to go out to dinner one evening, here is my card with my telephone number. Feel free to call."

> **Dr. Larkel Sherten**
> Professor of Computer Technology
> University of California, Riverside
> 909.555.1000

the card read.

Larkel's credentials made Kyra's heart skip two beats. She had never seen anyone as handsome as Larkel that was interested in teaching let alone actually partaking in the profession. What intrigued her more than his looks was his engagement in one of her career goals. Although Kyra had opened an architecture firm five years ago, she is halfway through her doctorate program and fully plans to stand in front of her own classes in a year's time. She plans to continue her business by day and teach at night.

Although she was embarrassed he had overheard a comment that she was making to herself, she didn't stop that from slipping the card into one of her bags as she took a seat to wait for her massage. She told herself she could not possibly call a complete stranger. That would automatically show desperation, and she did not want to appear needy.

Also, she was sorely reminded of the last blind date she had gone on. She had trusted the opinion of one of her friends and had gone out with a complete stranger, someone with whom her friend was newly acquainted. She had told her friend it was okay to give the guy her phone number. On the phone, he seemed nice enough, but when they met for dinner, it was a *completely* different story.

Not allowing guys to know where she lives, Kyra thought it would be best for them to meet at the restaurant. Upon her arrival, she looked for the blue striped sweater he said he would be wearing. First of all, she didn't expect the sweater to have a colorful peacock on the front. Secondly, she didn't expect a thirty-six year old professional man to have a Mohawk for his choice of hairstyle.

Everything in her told her to leave right then and there. But did she listen to herself? No! She proceeded to allow herself to be subjected to whatever the evening would bring.

As her date followed the host to the table, she slowly walked behind. All of a sudden, out of nowhere, she caught a whiff of cologne that reeked of something similar to Old Spice and Cool Water mixed together. She hoped the scent was coming from another patron that she had passed and not her date. She would not be able to bear that horrid smell from across the table all night.

When they reached their table, her date politely pulled out her chair. As Kyra began to take her seat, her date leaned into her and placed a moist kiss on her cheek. She could have sworn that she felt the tip of his tongue brush against her. She did not find this flattering at all, as they had just met five minutes ago. In the midst of her disgust, she smelled that horrid scent again, realizing it *was* her date that was wearing the deadly cologne.

Suffice it to say, the date didn't go well at all. Most of the dinner hour was filled with stories of her date's past relationships and baby momma drama. He was totally intrigued with himself and his life's accomplishments that he paid little attention to Kyra, except for when he complimented her here and there about her luscious lips and smooth silky skin that he wanted to lick like an ice cream cone.

At the end of dinner, Kyra quickly walked to her car and sped home, while her date was in the restroom. She felt like a character in a Batman movie who was making a quick getaway.

Later that evening, Kyra returned home feeling refreshed from her makeover. She popped some leftovers into the microwave and went into her bedroom to put aw0ay the new additions to her wardrobe. As she turned the Macy's bag upside down, Larkel's card fell onto the floor. She picked it up and laid it on her dresser. *No*, she told herself, *I can't. Absolutely not!*

When Kyra walked into her bathroom, a slight breeze came in from the bedroom window and swept the business card behind the dresser. But because Kyra had no intentions of calling Larkel, she didn't even miss the card. She never gave it a second thought.

Back in his newly remodeled home, Larkel sat down to review his plans for his upcoming computer courses. As he turned on his computer screen, the picture of the woman he used as a screensaver suddenly reminded him of the young woman he had seen in the mall earlier that day. He wondered what her name is. He knew he had let a wonderful opportunity pass when he settled for handing her his business card instead of asking her name and phone number. *But there is still a chance that she will call,* he thought.

Chapter Two

The next morning, Kyra walked down the hall of the administration building to the dean's office. She had to pick up the itinerary for the following week. She, along with the other graduate students who were preparing to begin interning, had to attend a special seminar that would give them the details of their assignments.

For the rest of the week, Kyra studied hard while preparing the final drafts of her term papers while trying hard not to let her thoughts linger too long on the impending seminar.

By the end of week, Kyra was exhausted and decided to spend the weekend indoors.

On Saturday morning, she pulled out her favorite movies, put on her favorite pair of cotton sweats, and curled up in her favorite chair. Although she laughed and cried as she watched *Lean on Me* and *Soul Food*, her mind kept wandering to the seminar. She was anxious to start her internship and was beginning to wonder about her assigned mentor. Would they get along, would he/she be helpful in overcoming any challenges she might face, and what type of personality would he/she possess?

Chapter Three

In a nearby city, an alarm could be heard going off at 6:30am. Larkel immediately stepped onto the cold, hardwood floor and made his way to the dresser to grab a pair of shorts and a tank. Every Saturday morning, he had a standing appointment at the gym. He worked out there after he jogged the four-mile distance between his home and the gym.

As he ran, he reminded himself to drop by the architecture firm a colleague had recommended to discuss plans for a new building. After having taught a variety of computer courses for UCR,

Larkel had always desired to have his own school, similar to ITT and DeVry. Now that he had received his inheritance from his father's estate, money was no longer an issue.

Once he returned home and had showered, he chose a cool pair of tan slacks and a thin beige sweater to wear to the architecture firm. When he arrived at the firm, he introduced himself to the secretary at the desk but was disappointed to find out that Kyra Fraser, the lead architect and owner, had taken the weekend off. His colleague had said she was definitely the one to discuss business with.

"I'd be more than happy to see if the other architect can assist you," Sandy, the office assistant, offered.

"No, thank you. But, is it possible to make an appointment with Ms. Fraser for Monday?"

"As a matter of fact, she has an open spot for a consultation right after lunch. Will you be available at one o'clock?"

"Yes, that fits my schedule. Oh, and may I leave my business card, so she can contact me if she has any questions beforehand?"

"I'll see that she gets it."

Although Larkel was disappointed because he was anxious to get started on his new adventure, he knew he still had work to do on his end. He still needed to secure a lot before the building could be constructed. Although not really anxious about this part of the project, Larkel dialed Century 21 to see if his application had been processed.

Chapter Four

Anxious to get to the office on Monday morning to meet with the three new clients and one prior client that Sandy had called to say she had appointments with, Kyra hurried through her breakfast and jumped into the shower. She decided to wear a hunter green pantsuit that not only had a professional look but a feminine appeal as well. She pulled her hair back into a twist that allowed small tendrils to fall about her almond-shaped face. After she lightly applied her makeup, she grabbed her briefcase and was ready to go.

As she pulled out of the driveway, she programmed Alicia Keyes, John Legend, and Kenny G into the cd changer. As she listened to the smooth, rhythmic tunes, her mind slowly wandered to her best friend whom she hadn't spoken to in several weeks. She had been so tied up with school that she hardly had any time for a social life. Also, the firm took up quite a bit of her time, especially since she was looking for a new third partner. The original third partner, Mark, had left to begin his own firm with his brother.

Although Kyra and Celeste could handle the new clientele and drafting the blueprints, it was always nice to have Mark around to oversee construction. She had to remember to check with Sandy to see if there had been any response to the ad they had placed in the paper last week. If so, she and Celeste planned to meet with potential partners together in order to make a final selection. This would mean she would need to spend more time at the firm in order to be available for the screenings. And although she values Celeste's opinions, she would have the final say because after all she is the owner and senior partner.

Walking into the office, it was always a delight to see her jovial, fun-loving office assistant Sandy.

"Good morning, Sandy."

"Good morning, Kyra. You looked refreshed and ready to take on the world. Maybe I need to get some rest and relaxation and come back looking like a million bucks."

Kyra blushed and waved away Sandy's comments. Sandy was always showering her with compliments and flattery. She treated her like a daughter, but with respect.

"Are there any messages?"

"They're all in your in-basket. I believe you have four."

Once Kyra was settled into her office, she reached into her in-basket and was surprised to see that Tracy, her best friend, had called. She hadn't spoken to her in a couple of weeks. After instructing Siri to make the call, she waited for Tracy to answer the phone.

"Hey girl. What's up?" Tracy practically screamed into the phone.

"All is well. How is everything going with you? How is James?"

"Well, I'm fine, but actually James is the reason I called."

Kyra could detect a little stress in Tracy's voice. "Well, what's wrong? Is he okay?"

"He's fine, but his job is doing layoffs, and he was laid off two days ago. Do you know any firms that have any positions open?"

"As a matter of fact I do. Wow, how ironic."

"What Kyra? What's going on?"

"Well, you remember Mark right?"

"The good-looking white boy that works there? Yeah, who could forget Mark with his nice biceps and tight butt."

"Tracy! Anyway, Mark doesn't work here anymore. He opened a firm with his brother."

"Ok, good for him, but what does that have to do with James?"

"Well, we haven't filled Mark's spot yet, and we will probably start having interviews this week."

"Kyra, would you seriously think about hiring James?"

"Well, Celeste and I are doing team interviews, so I would want to get her opinion. But remember, I've seen a few of the projects

James has worked on. They were pretty impressive."

"This will just make his day. He hasn't been himself lately you know with losing his job and..."

"And what, Tracy? Is there something else going on?"

"Yeah, Kyra. I'm pregnant."

"Oh girl, congratulations! I'm going to be an auntie? Why haven't you told me? How far along are you?"

"Girl, slow down. I just found out three days ago that I'm six weeks, but I didn't have a chance to call with everything going on with James."

"I understand. I guess everything is pretty overwhelming for you two right now. But everything will work out."

"So when can James come in?"

"Well, have him call Sandy and make an appointment."

"Kyra, we really appreciate this."

"No problem, girl. But on another note, you and I will have to get together soon."

"Just say where and when."

"I'll call you."

"Okay, bye for now."

After answering all her messages, Kyra decided to go down the hall and look in on Celeste. Kyra had met Celeste five years ago while working at another architecture firm. Celeste had interned for Kyra's boss and later came to work for Kyra last year.

Celeste was deeply engrossed in a file that was spread across her desk. She barely heard Kyra enter. "Why the serious look?" Kyra asked.

"Well, I'm looking at the figures for the Peterson project, and I'm triple checking to see if the accountant hasn't made a gross error."

"Why? Are we projected to be over budget?"

"No, not exactly," Celeste answered slowly. Kyra began to get a little irritated, so she moved closer to Celeste's desk.

"What do you mean not exactly? Either we're over budget or we're not."

Celeste slowly lifted her head from the papers and removed her glasses. "Well, according to these figures, we are well under budget, which means we stand to make a huge profit."

This concerned Kyra because they were never usually off target with the expenses. They used the same construction companies, material suppliers, and interior decorators for each project. Therefore, they were well aware of their price ranges and knew of their quality. "Let's schedule a meeting with Walker and Jones to discuss our planned budget for the Peterson project, and we'll go from there. There's no sense in speculating. I'm sure there is an obvious explanation."

After returning to her office and meeting with her first two appointments of the day, Kyra decided to relax and order lunch to be delivered. She moved from behind her desk, slid onto the plush leather couch and clicked on the TV. As she waited for her lunch to arrive, she wondered about her new client with whom she had an appointment at 1:00. *What was it that Sandy had said about him?* she thought.

Chapter Five

Just as Larkel was reaching for the phone to check for a message from Century 21, there was a knock on his office door. "Professor Sherten, are you busy?"

"No, come right on in. How can I help you?"

"Well, I'm having a problem understanding how asynchronous communication works."

"Well, if you come to my office about a half hour before our next class, I'll be happy to answer any questions you may have. Or, you can choose to go to the computer technology lab. The student assistants there should be able to help you because they've all had my class. Unfortunately, right now I'm on my way to an appointment."

Twenty minutes later, Larkel stepped out of the elevator on his way to *Diamond in the Rough Architecture Firm*. "Good afternoon. I have a one o'clock appointment with Ms. Fraser."

"Of course. I remember you from the other day, Mr. Sherten," Sandy replied. "Have a seat and I'll let her know that you're here."

Sandy couldn't keep from blushing as she walked to Kyra's office. Normally, she called from her desk to let Kyra and Celeste know of their clients' arrivals. But, today she wanted to make a special introduction. "Kyra, let me look at you."

"Why Sandy? What's wrong?"

"Oh nothing, but that handsome fella I was telling you about is sitting in the lobby," Sandy said as she surveyed Kyra from head to toe.

"You mean my one o'clock appointment?"

"Uh huh," Sandy answered absentmindedly.

"Sandy! You wouldn't be trying to play matchmaker again now would you?" Kyra complained.

"No, not necessarily, but it wouldn't help to go powder your nose."

"Sandy, just send him in."

As Kyra was placing the new edition of *Architecture Quarterly* on the bookcase behind her desk, she heard a tap at her door. "Come in," she said over her shoulder.

"Good afternoon, Ms. Fraser."

As Kyra turned around and saw the familiar face, she slowly extended her hand but didn't know what to say.

"You are Ms. Fraser, right?"

"Oh yes, but please call me Kyra."

"Kyra Fraser," Larkel said methodically.

"Yes, and you are?"

"Larkel Sherten."

"Nice to meet you, Mr. Sherten."

"Again," Larkel said with a smile.

"Excuse me?" Kyra remarked.

"You do recall meeting me about a week ago, don't you?"

"Well, we weren't formally introduced, but yes I do recall running into you at the health spa."

For a moment, they just sat there wondering what to say next. Finally, Kyra spoke up. "What brings you to *Diamond in the Rough Architecture Firm,* Mr. Sherten?"

"Please call me Larkel. I'm looking to start a computer technology school, and I'm looking for a reputable firm to do the construction, and your firm came highly recommended."

"Thank you. I appreciate the referral. Have you purchased the property where you want the building erected, or are you looking to renovate an existing structure?"

"Actually, I'm in the process of purchasing land now to have a brand new building erected. I'm expecting a call from Century 21. I put in a bid for a piece of land in Fontana."

"Well, until you have actually secured the property there isn't much I can do. It wouldn't be wise to start the blueprints without knowing the size of the lot, what the foundation currently consists of, and the other important factors as well."

Larkel hesitated a moment, then he asked, "Is it okay with you if I take a moment to call Century 21? They may have the answer I'm looking for."

"Sure. I'll give you some privacy."

Kyra decided to walk to the front desk as she waited for Larkel to complete his call. "Well?" Sandy questioned.

"Well what?" Kyra asked innocently as she played dumb.

"What do you think of him?"

"Actually, we already met, sort of."

"He didn't mention that when he made his appointment," Sandy said, sounding confused.

"Well, it's a long story."

"Do I look like I'm going somewhere," Sandy laughed.

"No, I guess not. But, we'll talk later."

"I want all the details."

When Kyra walked back into her office, Larkel was reseated at her desk looking over a document that he had just received over his portable, wireless fax. She stood at the door and did a quick survey. She noticed that he was clean shaven, very well dressed, and his nails were clean and trimmed. She wondered if he got his nails manicured.

A few seconds later, she snapped out of it and cleared her throat as she walked in. "I see you're all finished with your call. How did things go?"

"Well better than I expected. No one else placed any bids before the deadline, so I got the property and with a $10,000 savings."

"Well, I guess congratulations are in order."

"Would you like to help me celebrate by having dinner with me tonight?"

"I don't like to mix my personal life with business. So, I will have to pass on the celebration. But, please know I am happy you were able to acquire the property you wanted."

"Thank you. Well, I guess we should begin discussing the plans," Larkel said with a hint of disappointment in his voice.

Kyra moved forward with discussing the plans for Larkel's dream tech center, and she tried hard to listen to his desires, but something inside of her was tugging at her. She really wanted to say yes to his invitation, but she just wasn't sure. She had heard too many horror stories about people mixing business and pleasure. And the outcome wasn't usually good. She decided to go with an air of caution.

Chapter Six

Thursday rolled around, and Kyra and Celeste were preparing to interview James. Kyra didn't mention to Celeste that she knew James personally because she wished to solicit an unbiased opinion about James that would help in making her final selection. They had already interviewed four other candidates in the last two days, and James would be their final interviewee.

"Mr. Talbert has arrived for his interview," Sandy said through the meeting room's intercom. "Send him in," Kyra responded. "Good afternoon,

Mr. Talbert. I'm Kyra Fraser, and this is Celeste McGee. Please, have a seat, and we'll get started."

Kyra and Celeste had previously agreed to withhold comments regarding the candidates until each one had been interviewed. After James' interview had been completed, they decided to discuss each candidate over lunch.

"Well, Miss Celeste. Do you want to go through the list or do you want to tell me your top two of the five?"

"Let's cut to the chase. If I tell you my top two and you give me yours, we can narrow them down faster."

"That's true. I was particularly impressed by Raymond Eli and James Talbert. I believe their experience speaks for itself."

"I agree that their resumes are impressive, but I was impressed by the Biltmore project that Shenell Brody worked on."

"Okay, and who is your second choice?"

"James Talbert."

"Good, at least we agree on one. That will make my decision easy."

"It sounds like you already made up your mind."

"Well, I have now, with your support."

"So is James Talbert our man?"

"In a manner of speaking, yes. But, actually he's my best friend's husband."

"Why didn't you mention that?"

"Well, I wanted to be as unbiased as possible."

"No nepotism, hunh?"

"Yeah, something like that."

When Kyra arrived home that night, she had a message from Tracy and James thanking her from the bottom of their hearts for James' new position. Now that she had that issue settled, she could focus on her internship and find out why they were so under budget on the Peterson project.

Settling in for the night, Kyra went into the kitchen to make herself a cup of tea. She always found chamomile tea soothing; it helped her to fall easily into a deep sleep. She would need it for the busy day she had scheduled tomorrow.

Once again, her mind went back to her newest client- Larkel Sherten. She was so intrigued by him. It wasn't just his muscular build or his deep sexy voice. It was his level of professionalism and his level of academic achievements all rolled up into one sexy hunk of a man. She wondered if her 'no mix of business and personal' policy would cause her to lose out on something wonderful in her life.

It had been a while since she had dated anyone, and she was ready for a change. But she would not settle for just anyone. She felt her time was too precious to waste. If she were to date, it would not be for the simple purpose of having someone to go out with. No, it had to be deeper than that.

She decided to call Tracy to get her input on the situation. After Tracy's phone rang twice, Kyra heard her lively voice on the other end.

"Hey Ky. I guess you received our message?"

"Yes, I did. Please tell James he is welcome, but there really is no need to thank me. His experience speaks for itself. But hey. That's not why I called. I need your opinion."

"Oh yeah? About what?"

"I met a guy at the mall last week, and he gave me his card and said I should call sometime. I didn't call him, but then he showed up in my office."

"What do you mean he showed up in your office? How did he know where your office is? Is he some kind of stalker, Ky?"

"Wait slow down, Trace! When he came to my office, he did not know he was coming to see me. He didn't even know my name. He came on a referral."

"How do you know that? That sounds too coincidental to me."

"Tracy, stop being so suspicious. He was just as surprised to see me as I was to see him when he walked into my office. I could tell by the look on his face."

"Okay. Let's say what you are saying is true. What's your concern?"

"Thank you for letting me get to my point. He came to my office for me to build a technology center for him. He was given some good news while he was in my office, and he asked me to go to dinner with him to celebrate. I told him I don't mix business with pleasure. But I am really having second thoughts."

"Well, what is your gut telling you?"

"My gut is saying, 'Don't miss this opportunity.'"

"Well, I agree with your gut. If everything that you know about him is intriguing you, it may be worth finding out."

"Yeah, I don't mind finding out. My biggest concern is what if things between us go sour and we still have to work together. What then?"

"Just try to think positively. Take things slowly. Explain your position to him and come to an agreement beforehand. Feel him out a little before you make a decision."

"Thanks, Trace. I knew you would be the voice of reason."

"Does that mean you are going to call him?"

"No, it doesn't mean that. But, I will probably give it a try. I will see him soon. I will wait for him to ask again. If he is really interested, he'll ask again."

"I'm sure he will. Talk to you later."

"Good night."

Feeling better after having spoken to her best friend, Kyra rewarmed her tea, drank it, and called it a night.

Chapter Seven

Thank God, it's Friday. Now, I can finally begin my internship. Having James on board will free up some of my time. There has to be a parking spot somewhere on this campus. I swear, if I didn't have the new cd from Devo Called and Chosen with his number one hit single "You've Been So Good," I would probably commit road rage. Actually, all of the songs are spectacular. Devo's tunes have a calming effect as he reminds his listeners of God's grace and mercy. Hey, I'm no preacher, but I know how to keep a healthy balance in this world we live in. Oh, finally a parking spot. Driving around for ten minutes can cause a person to be late.

After finding a parking spot, Kyra ran into the building, located the correct classroom, and slid into a seat just as the professor began to speak.

"Welcome everyone. I'm assuming everyone is here to get information on your internship and is anxious to get started. Right?"

That's an understatement. I'm anxious to get started and finished, Kyra thought.

"Why don't we go around the room and introduce ourselves? Some of you will be working together, so it would be nice if we get to know one another. I'll begin. I'm Rebecca Lunsford. I completed my doctoral studies in the late 70's and have been teaching doctoral level courses since the mid 80's. Before that, I taught for 25 years and was in administration for six. Who wants to volunteer to go next?"

I may as well get this over with. "Hello, everyone. I'm Kyra Fraser, and I am an architect and the proud owner of *Diamond in the Rough Architecture Firm*. I have been involved with various levels of architecture for the past seven years since I earned my bachelor's degree.

During that time, I earned my master's degree, and I am anxious to complete this doctoral program because I want to teach others about architectural design courses."

After all the other numerous introductions of Andrea, Keiki, Izabel, Stephanie, Chuck, Bernadine, and Richard, Kyra was exhausted from listening. Ironically, she was paired with Keiki and Stephanie who share her career and educational interests. The three of them were assigned to the computer technology department because they all desire to teach with the use of electronic media.

Now that that is settled, off to the office I go. I am anxious to hear what Walker and Jones have to say about the figures on the Peterson project. All I know is they better not be cutting corners. My name is behind every building that we construct, and I will not sacrifice that just to make a buck. I wonder if they ordered lunch in at the office; I'm starving.

Kyra quickly directed Siri to call Sandy at the office to get an update on the day's activities.

"Sandy, have you and the two-man crew eaten lunch?"

"Actually boss, we were just about to send out for Chinese food. Should I order enough for you?"

"Yes, thank you. I should be there inside of twenty minutes. Do I have any urgent messages?"

"None that are pressing. However, Mr. Sherten did call. He asked that you give him a call right away. Something you might want to share?"

"No, there is nothing to share. I will return his call and see what he needs."

"He probably needs you!" Sandy said with a sadistic laugh.

"Well, I'm sure it's about business. I'll see you when I get there, Sandy."

"Kyra, you really need to loosen up. Live a little."

I don't know what to think. I wonder if he has changed his mind about working with the firm because I rejected his celebration proposal. Some men don't deal with rejection well. Well, I guess I won't know until I return his call.

"Hello, Larkel?"

"Yes. How may I help you?"

"This is Kyra Fraser. I'm returning your call."

"Hello, Kyra. Thank you for getting back to me. How is your day going?"

"It's going well actually. How about yours?"

"I have no complaints. Let me get to why I called. This evening, I need to go by and sign documents for the property I purchased. I elected to do that at the site. I would very much appreciate it if you could ride over with me, so you can see the lot for yourself."

"I have a two o'clock appointment. What time is yours?"

"I don't need to be there until four. Will you be done by then?"

"Yes, my meeting shouldn't take more than thirty minutes. Where should I meet you?"

"The lot is located on the corner of Cherry and Foothill Blvd. But, I can pick you up if you like."

"That would be nice. So, I'll see you around 3:30?"

"I look forward to seeing you at 3:30."

When Kyra disconnected from the phone call, her heart began to flutter. She had not felt that kind of excitement in such a long time. She was definitely intrigued by this man who suddenly- out of no where- appeared into her life.

Making it safely to the office, she joined the others for lunch in the spacious kitchen.

Lunch was great, or either I was just hungry. Walker and Jones should be here any minute, Kyra thought as she wiped her mouth.

"Kyra, Walker and Jones are here."

"Thanks, Sandy. Show them into conference room number one, and page Celeste. And I'll be right there."

Almost skipping into the conference room, Kyra greeted the men, "Good afternoon, Walker. Hello, Jones. How are my two favorite gentlemen?"

"Just fine, thank you, Kyra. And Celeste, it's good to see you as well."

"Okay, gentlemen. Let's get started. We have some serious concerns about the Peterson project. According to our records and the estimates that you sent over, we are far under our projected budget. Can you explain the discrepancy?"

"I'm glad you asked. That is one thing that we had planned to discuss with you and our other clients as well."

"So, it's not just this firm that this is affecting?"

"No. All of our clients stand to make profits for the next several months."

"And why is that?"

"Our number one material supplier is going out of business and is offering all final merchandise at a discounted rate. Therefore, we stand to save a great deal of money, and we are passing that savings on to you. Once they go out of business, it's no telling who will be our next supplier and if the products will take an increase in price."

"Okay, now things are beginning to make sense. Do you have any concerns, Celeste?"

"Well, I have one question. Have you begun to get quotes from other companies?"

"Actually, we have. We have a few more references to check out. Once we have that done, we will send you over a list, and you can make your selection."

"Thank you, I appreciate you doing the leg work. That saves a lot of time."

"Well, we are just as concerned about the quality of the material as you are. Remember our company name is at stake as well."

"Thank you gentlemen for coming down and clearing up these issues. It definitely puts our minds at ease."

Now that that's settled. I can get ready for the trip over to the lot with Larkel. Let me grab my skirt and make-up bag out of the car, so I can freshen up. It's a good thing I went by the cleaners today. Now, I have something clean and fresh to put on after a long day of work and meetings.

Chapter Eight

When Kyra exited the building, a gentle breeze blew past her. Her hair blew back revealing the soft features of her face and her large wide eyes. As Larkel exited his car, right in the entryway, he couldn't take his eyes off her. When Kyra looked up and saw him standing there, leaning against his car, her heart skipped two beats. There was something about this man that was very moving. He was so handsome and smooth. She really didn't know what to make of him.

"Wow, you look great."

"Thanks, Larkel. So do you."

"No, really. That caramel-colored sweater really brings out the honey color in your skin. You look radiant."

"Thank you, I appreciate the compliment," Kyra replied, openly blushing and showing all teeth.

"Okay. Don't forget we're going to a dirt lot, so be careful with your suede shoes."

"Thank you, Larkel. You are so considerate, but I have that covered. I have a pair of fully enclosed shoes in my bag."

"Yeah, I forgot. This is your line of business. Let me get your door for you."

"Oh, I see we have the same tastes in vehicles," Kyra said as she walked around to the passenger side of Larkel's car.

"Do you like the Jaguar XJL?"

"Yes, it's actually my dream car. When this model was created a couple of years ago, I had a newfound interest in the Jag."

"Okay, so when are you going to make your dream become a reality?"

"I don't know. I guess I'm just not ready for the bill yet."

"I know what you mean. But it doesn't appear that it would be an issue for you."

"It probably wouldn't be, but before Jaguar created that car, I had just bought my Mercedes. So, I'm just being satisfied with it. But, we will see what happens in the near future. I definitely plan to get one."

Larkel and Kyra took the short drive while making small talk. As he drove, she tried desperately to keep her eyes on the scenery around her, but her eyes kept traveling back to his side of the car. Each time she glanced over at him, she noticed he was looking in her direction as well. The excitement was really churning in her stomach. She almost felt like a cheerleader in high school who had a crush on the star quarterback. But, actually, it was just the normal feelings a woman has for a man.

"Here we are," Larkel announced as he pulled onto the dirt lot.

"I remember when this property went on the market. Wasn't that about three or four months ago?"

"Actually, it's been a little longer than that."

"This is a great spot for a business. I'm surprised it took so long to sell. Maybe they wanted too much for it."

"Well, they did want a pretty penny, but I'll bet it's worth every dime."

"I'll take your word for it."

"Do you want to wait here while I sign the docs or do you want to walk over with me?"

"Actually, I came so I could look around the lot. I will just walk around and take notes. That will give you some privacy while you handle your business."

"I appreciate that, but I don't mind your company. I'll make it quick."

While waiting for Larkel, Kyra walked around the massive lot. Finally, she returned to the car and changed her shoes again. Kyra leaned her head back against the soft leather of the comfy seat, and after a few minutes, she fell asleep even though she was only trying to rest her eyes.

After Larkel signed his docs, he returned to his car to find Kyra resting comfortably. He quietly opened the car door and slid into his seat. For a moment, he just took in Kyra's beauty. He found himself to be so drawn to her. Finally,

Larkel reached over and touched Kyra's shoulder to gently wake her. "Hey Kyra. Are you hungry?"

"A little, I guess," Kyra asked as she straightened up in her seat and opened her eyes.

"There is a very nice restaurant not too far from here. Maybe we can grab a quick bite."

Kyra consented and off they went.

When they arrived at the restaurant, Larkel quickly walked around the car and opened Kyra's door. He then took her arm and almost lifted her out of the car. Kyra felt her body go warm as if though she was going to melt inside.

Walking into the restaurant, Kyra exclaimed, "Larkel, this is such a beautiful restaurant. It has nice ambiance."

"Have you ever been here before?"

"Actually, I came here once about a year ago. But, I don't remember it being this beautiful."

"Well, I think this place is appropriate."

"What do you mean?"

"A beautiful place for a beautiful woman."

"Thank you," Kyra responded blushing again.

Because Larkel had made a reservation as soon as he had Kyra's consent, they were able to be seated right away. After they made their selection for their meal and drinks, Larkel continued their conversation. "So, Kyra, tell me a little about yourself."

"What exactly do you want to know?"

"Well, I already know that you own an architecture firm and that you are almost done with your doctorate degree. What else is there to know about the beautiful young lady that sits across from me? Do you have any deep dark secrets that you want to reveal? Any bones sticking out of your purse?"

"Okay, okay. I think I get the picture. First of all, everyone has secrets. But, I don't think I'll reveal any of mine tonight though. You, however, can feel free to spill the beans."

"Sounds like you're being a little evasive."

"No, not really. I feel awkward when someone asks me about myself. I feel like I'm on display. I feel if we have the basics down, then we can go from there. I'm not about playing games. Well, actually I love games. But the mind games I can do without. I'm pretty straight forward with what I feel and what I want."

"I understand what you're saying…"

"Hold on, please. I'm not finished. Let me answer your question. I'm thirty years old, independent, and very much motivated. I am enthusiastic about life, and I look at each day as a new challenge, an opportunity to get something accomplished. I love to help those that are less fortunate that I am. Basically, I'm a giver. And on that note, I'll *give* you an opportunity to tell me a little about you."

"Hold that thought. I need to wash my hands. I'll be right back."

Talk about being put on the spot. I guess I should have expected that. People always share information about themselves on a first date. Did I say 'first date?' Maybe I'm a little rusty. Or maybe I'm just a little cautious. Anyway, I'm having a great time so far. I didn't even mind when he held my hand. Usually, I don't like it when people who are unfamiliar touch me, especially my hands. But his hand was so warm and inviting. And his beautiful brown eyes are to die for. Not to mention that killer smile. I just wanted to reach over and see if his lips...

"Kyra? Are you okay?

"Hunh? Oh yeah, sorry."

"Where was your mind?"

"Actually, I was just thinking of you."

"Oh, really? What were you thinking about?"

"I'm just interested in knowing more about you. It's your turn remember?"

"Yes, but before I start I have something for you." Larkel pulled a long-stemmed red rose from behind his back that he had quickly purchased from a vendor right outside the door of the restaurant.

"Oh, a rose. It's beautiful. I love roses."

"I figured that. I saw the ones you had on your bookcase. It looked like you could use a fresh one. Our food is here. I'll fill you in on me while we eat."

"I'm ready. But don't tell too many broken-hearted stories. I can only take so many skeletons in one day."

"I hope you aren't implying that I've broken hearts. In all honesty, I probably have broken one or two, but not intentionally. Sometimes when we are young, we make stupid mistakes. But hopefully as we grow, we get wiser. I'm 33 and single. I was married five years ago, but we decided that splitting up was the best for us. We didn't have any kids, so we didn't have to worry about causing any psychological damage to anyone other than ourselves. Since the divorce, I've thrown myself into my career and after my father's death two years ago, I decided to open a technology center but just got around to focusing on it. If you don't mind me asking, are you single, Kyra?"

"Yes, I am, and I've never been married."

"So here we are."

"Here we are."

After pausing for a moment, Larkel decided to take a chance while he had Kyra's full attention.

"There's a beautiful place that I would love to show you if you are not in a hurry to get home."

"Actually, I'm not working this weekend, so I'm not in a rush to get home."

"Do you alternate working on weekends or do you take off or work as needed?"

"I have been working quite a few weekends for the last couple of months because we were down one partner. But now since that problem is solved, I'll have more time to do other things."

"Am I on the 'other-things' list?" Larkel asked with a sly look in his eyes.

"Well, I did originally tell you that I do not like to mix business with my personal life. But, I may be willing to set that rule aside for now, as long as we don't let anything spoil our professional relationship. So, to answer your question, I guess time will tell if you're on that list or not," Kyra answered with a smile as she put a fork full of lobster tail in her mouth, as she wondered if the two of them seeing each other socially would be disastrous.

After dinner, Larkel drove Kyra down to the promenade in Long Beach to share an evening stroll. Many of the shops were still open, so they walked through and admired the various trinkets the merchants were hoping they would buy. Nothing appealed to either one of them, until they came to the candy shop and Kyra spotted the caramel apples.

"Oh wow, caramel apples," Kyra said with eyes as big as a kid's.

"Would you like one?" Larkel asked.

"Yes, but I prefer to have it sliced with the caramel drizzled over the top."

"One order of sliced caramel apples for the lady, please," Larkel ordered.

The couple found a cozy bench to sit on, so Kyra could enjoy her apples. Although Larkel himself doesn't really care for caramel, he couldn't resist letting Kyra share her treat with him from time to time. It would have been enjoyable for him just to watch her enjoy herself, but he enjoyed the moment of intimacy of eating from one dish.

After Kyra had her fill of the apples, they continued to enjoy the scenery and the beautiful moonlight hitting the water.

As they ventured out onto the sand, Kyra took her shoes off, so she could feel the cool sand between her toes, plus she did not want to ruin the suede Armani shoes she had recently splurged on.

Not being able to contain himself any longer, Larkel gently turned Kyra towards him and drew her petite frame close to his. He looked into her eyes as if he had done so a thousand times before.

"Are you enjoying yourself tonight?" he asked while continuing to look deep into her eyes.

"Yes. I am. I could not have asked for a better night. Thank you for everything."

"The pleasure is all mine," Larkel responded as he leaned in and kissed her. As he held his hand tightly against the small of her back, he felt the firmness of her body. Kyra didn't resist. She just went with the flow as she felt the excitement rise within her.

Just as gently as he had turned her, Larkel released her and softly whispered, "Let me get you back to your car. I don't want to keep you out too late."

Kyra was on a cloud. All she could do was nod.

Chapter Nine

I think last night was a successful first date, even if it wasn't a planned first date. Kyra seemed to have enjoyed herself at the promenade. The moon provided just enough light to mix in with the softly dimmed lights that were placed around the edge of the beach. That set a very romantic and playful mood. She's a lot of fun to be around. She has the same type of humor I do. She had me laughing so hard, I thought I'd bust a stitch. And the way she went crazy over the sliced caramel apples was nice to see. Her eyes lit up, and her smile is so pretty. I just wanted to continue kissing her as we stood on the beach, but I didn't want her to get the wrong idea about my intentions. It was good to see her be free and enjoy herself, and I didn't want to spoil the mood. I wonder what our next adventure will be. I have to come up with something nice. I think I have the perfect idea. I'll present it to her when I see her today.

So much for a day off. Well, I guess even though this is technically work, it could be considered play. Larkel wants to meet and begin the drafts for the building. I'm actually looking forward to seeing him again so soon. Last night was a blast. I think I may have overdone it with the caramel apples though. But they were so good and the caramel reminded me of his skin. I need to get myself under control. I was probably blushing like a schoolgirl. Oh, well. I guess he was just pushing the right buttons. And that kiss! That was really unexpected, but nice. And he didn't come on too strong. I wonder if I'm the only one who had to take a cold shower before I went to bed. And I hate cold water, but I needed to cool my body temperature down after I made it home last night. My, my, my. Mr. Larkel Sherten! What can I say?

As Kyra walked into the firm, a strange vibe came over her. *Why is the office so dark? Where is everyone? Is today the day everyone is off? Where is my mind? You would think I would know what was going on at my own company, but that's what Sandy gets paid for. I'll just check her calendar and see what's going on. Looks like Sandy is off, but James and Celeste should be here. Let me check the back office.*

"Celeste? James? Hello?" *Where are they? What is that noise?*

"Oh, Kyra! What are you doing here? I thought you were off today," Celeste asked, obviously surprised and annoyed to see Kyra.

"I was Celeste. But Mr. Sherten wants to get started on his plans. Where is James?"

"I'm right here, Ky. What's up?" James asked as he emerged from the dark office.

"Is everything okay? Why are the lights off?"

"Oh, we were just going over the plans for the Peterson project."

"I thought you guys finalized that last week."

"Well, I just wanted to bring James up to speed on the moderations that were made."

"I'll be in my office if you guys need me," Kyra retorted as she abruptly turned away from them.

"Actually, I think we're done here. Right, James?"

"Uh, yeah. I need to get home."

That was awfully suspicious. I hope Celeste isn't up to her old tricks. I know she has been single for a while, but she knows James is married to my best friend. Well, let me not jump to assumptions. I need to concentrate on the project at hand. Larkel will be here soon. Let me see what we have to drink in the fridge. I'm sure he would like something cold to drink.

As Kyra leaned over to look in the refrigerator, something caught her attention from the corner of her eye. Kyra quickly stopped her drink search and nearly put her entire face into the trashcan to get a closer look. *Is that a condom in the trashcan? What kind of nasty stuff is going on here?* She dared not touch the thin plastic object. As she moved closer, she realized the item was a sandwich bag. *I am really getting paranoid about the two of them.*

"Hello? Kyra, are you here?"

"Oh, I'm sorry, Larkel. I'm back here in the kitchen. I will be right there."

"Why are all the lights off?"

"I forgot to turn them on when I walked in. I was wondering the same thing."

"What do you mean? Aren't you here alone?"

"I am now. When I got here all the lights were off, but James and Celeste were here."

"Sounds like a little romance is going on in the office," Larkel said with a deep chuckle.

"Actually, that's not funny."

"Why not? They're both consenting adults, right?"

"That's not the point. James is married to Tracy, who just happens to be my best friend," Kyra replied showing her irritation.

"Oh, I'm sorry. I didn't know."

"I know you didn't. But that's why I'm hoping that where my mind is taking me is not what's really going on. Anyway, are you ready to get down to business?"

"As ready as I'll ever be."

"Are you hungry? I can order Chinese food from the place down the street. It's really tasty."

"Okay, you don't need to do a mini commercial. You sold me on the word 'hungry'."

"Oh, I see you have jokes early in the afternoon."

"Just trying to keep a smile on your face and take your mind off your partners."

"Well, you don't have to try hard, and I've already forgotten about them. What do you want to eat?"

"How about broccoli with beef or black pepper chicken or orange chicken?"

"Black pepper chicken is my favorite. Do you want steamed rice, fried rice, or Chow Mein?"

"Chow Mein."

"Great, I'll make the order, and it should be here in a half an hour. If you like you can walk down the hall to the lounge and help yourself to something to drink in the fridge. I'm sure Sandy stocked up before she left for the weekend."

"How is Sandy? Doesn't she usually work on Saturdays?"

"Yes, but her husband and kids took her away to go camping."

"That sounds like fun. That reminds me. Would you like to go to the spa with me?"

"The one in the mall?"

"No, I mean a real spa. I was thinking Glen Ivy."

"That sounds like fun. I've never been there."

"Well, you are in for a treat. What day is good for you?"

"Well, my week is flexible. I don't begin my internship for another week, and I don't have many clients scheduled for this week. All the projects are well underway, except for yours. So, I guess I better get down to business. How's your schedule?"

"I have classes on Tuesdays and Thursdays."

"Is the spa open on Mondays?"

"They're open seven days a week. Monday will be fine. Is ten o'clock good for you?"

"Sure, ten sounds great."

"You'll need a bathing suit, sun block, and oil or lotion."

Just when Larkel finished explaining the set up of the spa and the various activities, Kyra's office phone rang.

"Excuse me, Larkel, let me catch the phone. Hello? Hi, Tracy. What's up girl?"

"Hey, Ky. Is James there? He said he had to work today."

"He was here when I got here, but he left about half an hour ago. He said he had to go home."

"Well, he hasn't made it here yet. Maybe he's on his way. I didn't know that this job was going to require so much of his time. He's putting in a lot more hours than at his last job."

"He shouldn't be working more than thirty-five to forty hours a week. There's nothing too strenuous right now."

"Well, he seems to be putting in more like sixty."

"I don't know what to tell you, Tracy. But, none of us have been working crazy hours since James has been here. I'm going to need to call you back. I need to begin the Sherten project."

"Okay, Larkel are you ready to begin?"

"Sure. Let's get the show on the road."

"Explain to me how you want everything situated, what street you want the building to face, how many classrooms, offices, restrooms, number of floors, number of exterior entrances and exits...."

"Wow, I don't think I thought about all of that. I imagined the exterior and the large computer room and my office."

"Well, that's a start. How did you imagine the exterior would look?"

"I would like it to be primarily glass, some clear and some mirrored. Also, I would like the base to be gray brick. The inside flooring should be marble. I want two floors. The classrooms will be downstairs and the offices and meeting rooms will be upstairs."

"Sounds like you gave it a little thought."

"Yeah, maybe a little."

"What is the exact size of the lot? And how much do you want apportioned to parking?"

"It is three and a half acres. I think at least one acre should be designated for parking. What do you think?"

"That's about right. One-third of the property should be used for parking."

Kyra and Larkel worked intensively for hours on the design of his new building. Kyra enjoyed seeing the sparkle in Larkel's eye as they discussed various features of the building and construction process. Before long, hours had slipped away.

"What time is it, Larkel?"

"It's about 4:30. We've been here for over four hours."

"I know. Do you want to continue or do you want to take a copy of the sketches home and see if you want to make any alterations on either level or the parking lot before we continue?"

"Actually, I think you've done enough work for today. I know you were supposed to have the day off. I really appreciate you giving up your Saturday. I hope I didn't spoil any plans that you had."

"No, I probably would have just relaxed at home, driven down to San Diego to visit my cousin Vanessa, or gone to hang out with my friend Andrea if she wasn't working. I wish she would slow down some. I guess I don't really have room to talk. In some ways, I'm a workaholic myself. But, I really enjoy what I do. It doesn't even seem like work to me, most of the time. Not to mention that I have enjoyed your company for the last two days."

"I've enjoyed yours to. I'm glad you decided to accept this project. I'm very impressed with what you've done so far, and you've done quite a bit in such a little time. But, to change the subject from work, would you like to go to dinner or take in a movie?"

"I'm not hungry just yet. But a movie sounds good. What of movies do you like?"

"Action and comedy, mostly. But I like just about anything. I know Denzel has a new movie out. Wesley should be due for another one soon too. He needs to make an action flick. I like the ones where he plays some type of law enforcement officer."

"I know. He needs to get back into that and leave *Blade* alone."

"You didn't like *Blade*?"

"It didn't intrigue me enough to watch it. I only saw portions of it. But I do want to see Denzel's new movie, the one with Mark Wahlberg."

"Yes, that's the one I'm talking about. It should be really good."

"Can you get the movie times? I'm going to freshen up a bit."

Larkel didn't reply. He just pulled out his phone and began a search as he watched Kyra saunter from the room.

Once they had made it to the theatre, Larkel found it hard to concentrate on the movie. He couldn't help but notice how comfortable they felt around each other. They seemed to flow smoothly together. They were very much in synch.

This is a good movie, but I can't let this opportunity pass by. I'm sitting here in a dark theatre with a beautiful woman. I wonder if I can slip in another little kiss like I did in the drafting room. Her lips are so soft. How can a brother resist?

Not being able to hold back, Larkel reached over and took Kyra's hand and squeezed it. They looked at each other. Larkel leaned in towards Kyra; she kissed him softly but quickly and resumed watching the movie, as if nothing had happened. All Larkel could do was smile. *I definitely like her style*, he thought.

Chapter Ten

Last night was great. I am really enjoying spending time with Larkel. He is great company.

While Kyra was deep in her thoughts there was a knock at the door. *I wonder who's at my door at nine o'clock in the morning, on a Sunday.*

"Hey, Tracy. What's up girl? What brings you this way?"

"I need to talk to you, Ky. It's about James."

"What's the problem?"

"I don't know. I'm hoping maybe you can help."

"You know I'll do what I can. Start at the beginning."

"Well, everything just seemed to be happening at the same time. James lost his job, I found out that I was pregnant, and James started hanging out more than usual."

"What do you mean hanging out?"

"Well, he doesn't always come home when he says he's going to. He comes and goes when he wants. Like yesterday, for example. After I spoke to you, he didn't come home for another two hours."

"Well, what did he say when he got there?"

"That's just the thing. He didn't say anything. I asked him where he had been, and he said at work. I told him I had called the office, but he was gone. He still didn't say anything. He just went into the bedroom and closed the door."

"I don't know exactly how you think I can help you."

"Well, has anything strange been going on? How has he been at the office?"

"I haven't noticed anything out of the ordinary. Well, except for yesterday."

"What do you mean? What happened yesterday?"

"When I got to the office the lights were off, but James and Celeste were in the back. I asked them what they were doing, and they said they were going over adjustments on the Peterson project. I found it a little strange, but I don't like to interfere in people's business, so I let it go."

"But one of the people in question is your best friend's husband," Tracy said raising her voice.

"I know sweetie. But let's not jump to any conclusions. Let's come up with a plan that will help us get to the truth but does not jeopardize anyone's relationship. I don't want to be in the middle of this. If there is a "this." I think it would be best if you work this out with James. If you feel the need to come up to the job and bring your husband lunch or have lunch with your best friend, feel free to pop in whenever you like. You know I have an open-door policy for my best girl. What do you think?"

"Well, I understand your position. I'll try your method. I don't want James to think I don't trust him, but right now I don't. Enough about me and my marital problems. What's going on in your life, Ky? Did you ever decide to go out with that new client? What is his name?"

"Yes, I did. We've gone out twice already. His name is Larkel, and he is a professor at UCR. We've had dinner, gone to the promenade, and to the movies. And Monday, we are going to a spa."

"Wow, that's exciting. He's not wasting any time is he? I'm so happy for you girl."

"Well, don't be prematurely happy. We've only been going out for a week."

"Well, that's how it all starts right?"

"I guess you're right. So, tell me about the baby and when you are due."

"I'm only two months, so I have a long time left. But, we are so excited. At first, we were scared because of the job situation. But everything is working out. Hopefully."

"Don't worry, Tracy. Everything will work out. Let's go get some ice cream. Let me throw something on."

Chapter Eleven

On Monday morning, Kyra was still riding on a cloud from the time she spent with Larkel on Friday and Saturday. After not getting much sleep over the weekend, she nearly overslept. Just as she finished putting her hair up, Larkel rang the doorbell. After greeting him with a warm kiss, they made their way to the spa. Cutting through much of the morning traffic, they were able to make it in about thirty minutes.

"Here we are. Welcome to Glen Ivy. Are you ready?"

"What do we do first, Larkel?"

"Well, we need to go change, and then we can take a dip in the Jacuzzi. The Jacuzzis are separate; they are inside the dressing rooms. So, if you like you can take a dip and then meet me here in about thirty minutes."

"That sounds great. I'll see you soon."

This water feels so good. How relaxing. It has been too long since I've felt anything this good. Today is a day without contracts to review, papers to write, sketches to draw, or contractors to negotiate with. I wonder how Celeste and James are making out. No, I don't mean making out. I mean doing. You know- how their days are going. Well, I'm not going to worry about them today. But what if Tracy should decide to drop in and catch them in a compromising position. I won't be there to stop her from going off or from hell breaking loose! But that's really not my problem, now is it? Girl, why can't you just enjoy your day and stop worrying about everything and everybody else?

I wish I could immerse my full body under the water like those other women. But, if I put this straight hair under this nice, warm water, I will come out looking like a bad-hair-day Barbie doll. I'm talking afro-puff city. I'm not saying anything is wrong with wearing one's hair natural. It's just not the look I'm going for today, especially when I just spent money to get my hair done a few days ago. So, I'll just sit here and look pretty.

After enjoying the pool's jets for about twenty minutes, Kyra's body began to relax. She leaned her head back slightly against the edge of the tub. Before long, she began to doze off. But an unfamiliar voice broke her sleep.

"Ma'am? Are you okay?"

Nearly jumping out of her skin, Kyra lifted her head to find an elderly plump, gray-haired woman leaning over her.

"Yes ma'am. I was just relaxing."

"Yes, I can see that. But you don't want your beautiful skin to begin to look like a prune from being in the water too long, do you?"

"Uh, probably not. Thanks," Kyra responded as she lifted herself from the Jacuzzi and wrapped her towel around herself. Quickly locating Larkel while laughing to herself, Kyra made her way over to the table where he was patiently waiting.

"Are you ready for a mud bath?" he asked.

"Uh, well," Kyra began, somewhat startled. "I can't really say that I've ever looked forward to a mud bath. But if you recommend it, let's go."

"Right this way, my lady," Larkel responded, full of enthusiasm and life.

After making their way to the mud pool, Larkel immediately commenced to placing the thick warm mud on Kyra's back. "Your skin feels like silk. Are my hands too rough?"

"No. That feels good. Am I going to get the pleasure of rubbing mud all over your muscles?"

"Sure, if you like."

"Well, you look like you're having so much fun. I would like to join in."

"Okay, do you want to start with my back?"

"No, actually I would like to start with your front, so I can see the look on your face as I rub this warm mud across your nice firm chest. Are you ready? Come on."

"Maybe you're having too much fun. You have a devilish look on your face."

"Oh, don't be scared of little old me. You're a big strong man. Come here."

"Okay, okay. Go ahead."

The couple spent nearly an hour rubbing mud on each other and having a lot of fun tossing mud around. Kyra made sure she warned Larkel about staying clear of her hair. He saw the look on her face as she spoke, and he knew she was serious. Finally, the mud had hardened on their bodies making it hard to move as freely as they had before, so Larkel suggested this part of their adventure come to an end.

"The showers are right over here. Let's go wash this stuff off."

"Yeah. I agree."

"This shower is a little cold. Is all the mud off my back, Kyra?"

"Yes, but you have a little on the back of your neck. Let me get it for you. Check me. Am I good to go?"

"From where I am standing, you are definitely good to go," Larkel said while clearly checking Kyra out from head to toe.

"Thanks. So are you," Kyra said while pretending not to notice his constant stare.

Normally, she did not like men undressing her with their eyes. It made her feel creepy. But this time around, she was enjoying the attention. Larkel's look was one of genuine interest and not perversion. The attention he gave her made her feel special. She had never had anyone look at her the way he was looking at her now. Snapping her back to reality, Larkel began to speak.

"Would you like something to drink? They have really good iced tea here."

"Yes, I'm a little thirsty."

"After we get the iced tea, I'll give you a full body massage if you like."

"Sure. Do you know what you're doing?"

"I'll let you be the judge of that. Lay down here. Tell me how this feels."

"Oh, yeah. I think you have convinced me. You are an absolute expert."

Feeling like the massage had just begun and missing getting her iced tea, Kyra heard Larkel's voice suddenly appear from what seemed like nowhere.

"Sweetie, it's time to go."

"Oh my goodness! Did I fall asleep?"

"Yes, and you were calling the cows home!"

"Was I snoring?"

"Yeah, a little."

"Why didn't you wake me? How long have I've been asleep?"

"About forty-five minutes. I figured you needed it, and you looked so peaceful. I was just enjoying watching you."

"The place looks deserted," Kyra observed.

"They close in about fifteen minutes."

"I guess I'd better rub the sleep out of my eyes and get a move on. You must have magic hands because the last thing I remember was you giving me a massage and saying something about getting a drink of iced tea."

"Oh yeah. Here it is. I grabbed one for you while you were sleeping."

"Thank you. You are so considerate."

"Well, you are definitely worth it."

Chapter Twelve

Early Tuesday morning, Kyra lay in bed reminiscing about her time with Larkel. She had definitely let down her guard and allowed someone to come into her life. After the bad breakup she had with Marcus, she just wasn't ready to get into another tailspin romance. It had been three years since their breakup, and Kyra was still very much on guard. Sure, she had had a blind date here and there, but her highly charged internal radar never let any of the guys past the starting line.

But here she was three dates later with Larkel, and she was enjoying every moment. She looked forward to their next adventure without hesitation.

Leaving home and driving to the office, Kyra listened to the morning news reports. Before long, she pulled into her personal spot and made her way into the firm with a smile on her face.

"Good morning boss. We need to talk."

"Good morning, Sandy. You mean to tell me that we have issues already. It's not even ten o'clock."

"Well, before we get started with any drama, how was your weekend?"

"It was absolutely wonderful. I went out to dinner, I saw a movie, I went to the promenade, and I went to the spa yesterday. All thanks to Larkel."

"My, my, my. Haven't we been busy?"

"Yes, we have. How was your weekend?"

"I had a marvelous time. It's been a long time since the whole family has been able to spend a whole weekend together. Since the kids have left home and started their own families, everyone's different schedules makes it hard to get in synch. So, I really treasure times like these," Sandy answered with watery eyes.

"It's good to hear that you enjoyed yourself. Everyone should take time off from time to time to enjoy life. So, pray tell, Sandy. What seems to be of major concern this morning?"

"Well, Kyra. I'm concerned about James and Celeste spending so much time alone together."

"They are working on the construction of the Peterson project."

"I know, but it's more than that. I can't really put my finger on it. It's a feeling that I have. It seems like every time I turn around, Celeste is in James' office with that silly grin on her face. And haven't you noticed her change in dress?"

"I know where you are going with this, Sandy, and I can't say that the thoughts haven't crossed my mind. But, let's not be too hasty with our prejudgments. What is on my calendar for today?"

"Mr. Sherten is scheduled for three to go over the preliminary drafts."

"Is that it?"

"Yes, for now."

"Okay, I'll be in my drafting room adding in a few options for Larkel."

Kyra placed her personal items in her office and made her way to her drafting room, without stopping in to say good morning to James or Celeste, which was her usual routine. She did not want to witness anything she would be compelled to tell her best friend.

After getting started with the updates on the Sherten project drafts and working for a couple of hours, Sandy's booming voice came in loud and clear over the intercom.

"Kyra, Tracy is here and lunch just arrived also. Do you want me to place it in one of the conference rooms?"

"Can you place it in my office, Sandy? And tell Tracy to go right in. I'll be right there."

Surveying her closest friend from head to toe, Kyra greeted Tracy with her customary greeting.

"Hey, girlfriend. You're looking good."

"Thanks girl. So are you. I stopped by James' office on the way in, but he's not there. He did come in this morning, right?"

"Yes, girl. Don't get all paranoid on me. He left to go to the Peterson site."

"What about Celeste?"

"She's in her office."

"Good."

"Have a seat and let's eat."

"I'm starving. So, tell me about the rest of your weekend after I left Sunday morning."

Kyra filled her best friend in on her latest adventure with Larkel as they ate lunch.

At three pm sharp, Kyra's private line rang.

"Kyra, Mr. Sherten has arrived, and he is anxiously waiting your arrival in your drafting room."

"Thanks, Sandy. I'll be right there. Can you make sure that the beverages are warm and ready?"

"It's already been taken care of."

"How I love efficiency," Kyra beamed as she stood up to walk to meet Larkel down the hall. All of a sudden, she felt butterflies take flight in her stomach.

"Good afternoon, Kyra. You're looking as lovely as ever."

"Thank you, Larkel. How are you feeling today?"

"All is well. I slept really good last night after the spa treatment."

"So did I. Are you ready to get down to business?"

"Here?"

"Don't be funny! You know what I mean!"

"I know. I just thought I would throw that in. But, seriously I looked over the drawings, and I do have a couple of questions about additional white boards and a LCD projector that I would like to add into each room."

"We can definitely add those items in, but they would be attended to at a later stage of the construction process. I do have a couple of suggestions myself though. Tell me what you think about these."

"I'm sorry to interrupt, Kyra. But, I need to discuss an issue that just arose on the Monroe project."

"Come on in, Celeste. I'm not sure if you had the opportunity to meet Mr. Sherten. He is our newest client. He recently purchased the property on Cherry and Foothill, in Fontana."

"No, I haven't. Good afternoon, Mr. Sherten. It's nice to meet you."

"It's nice to meet you, also."

"Kyra, can you come into my office, so I can give you an update on the Monroe project?"

"Sure, I'll be right there. Give me three minutes. Larkel, excuse me for a moment while I check on another project. While I'm gone, take a look at the additions I made to the sketches."

Quickly walking down the hall to meet with Celeste, Kyra noticed she was rushing, so she could return to Larkel. She didn't want to be away from him too long. Although she had spent a great deal of time with him just the day before, she had already begun to miss him later that evening.

"Okay, Celeste. What seems to be the problem?"

"Monroe's check did not clear, and we sent it through twice. I've tried calling him, and I've left messages, but I haven't received any return calls. What is our next step? I don't recall ever having to deal with this before."

"Let me try to make a call or two."

Kyra immediately went into her office and closed the door behind her. She picked up the phone and dialed Monroe on his private cell. He answered after one ring. Discussing the tenuous issue with him sternly and quickly, the issue was resolved. After only three minutes, she was walking back down to the conference room with much pep in her step.

"I'm sorry, Larkel. Oh, Celeste. Thanks for keeping Mr. Sherten occupied while I took care of the Monroe issue. He will be stopping by to deliver a cashier's check. Meanwhile, all work all the project is to cease until further notice."

"I'll put the cease order in right away. It was nice talking to you, Mr. Sherten."

"She sure is friendly," Larkel said after Celeste left the room.

"Yes, I know. She didn't make you uncomfortable did she?"

"Not really. She just asked a bunch of questions about my project, and she took a look at the designs with me."

"Were they to her approval?" Kyra asked with a bit of sarcasm.

"There sounds like a bit of tension in your voice. Why is that? Is there bad blood between the two of you?"

"No, I wouldn't call it that. Celeste is beginning to make a reputation around here for herself. She has gone out with several clients, and she has no problem with going after someone's man."

"Oh, I see. And after the incident with her and James, I can see why you may be a little tense."

"Well, even though Tracy is my best friend and I would go to the end of the earth for her, I can deal with the situation with her and James a little better than Celeste sniffing around in my territory."

"Oh, so I'm your territory now?"

"I don't mean to sound possessive and to make you sound like cattle, but I thought we were beginning to develop something here."

"Don't get me wrong, I like the idea of being 'your territory' as you put it. And believe me, I have no interest in playing you and Celeste against each other."

Chapter Thirteen
(Five months later)

After waiting for her guests to finish greeting one another and take their seats, Kyra made her way to the podium to set the pace for the evening. She had reserved a private room at one of the local restaurants for this occasion.

"I want to thank all of you for coming tonight. I wanted to take the time to do something extra special for all of the partners, employees, and the construction crews. I truly believe that people don't say 'thank you' enough in this world. All of you are a valuable asset to this company, and I couldn't have done it without you. So, from the bottom of my heart I thank you. After dinner is ordered, served, and devoured, I will make my special presentations. So, enjoy yourself and order whatever you want from the menu; it's my treat."

This is a lot of fun. I really like get-togethers. It's good to have Larkel here with me. Things have been going great between us. My internship is done and graduation is coming up in a month. Soon, I'll be known as Dr. Fraser. Wow! Mom and Dad are so proud. Every time I think of it, I just want to cry. Happy tears, of course.

Tracy's pregnancy is coming along fine, which is a miracle with all the stress she's under. James is still acting weird. And Miss Celeste, well who knows about her these days.

We have completed the Peterson project and the Monroe project. The Sherten and Taylor projects are in their final stages. And, we have three new projects under our belts.

God has truly been good to Diamond in the Rough Architecture. *We even made it into the two latest issues of* Architecture Quarterly *with the*

Steinberg and Monroe projects being featured. I'm hoping that Larkel's project makes it in as well. His building has a very unique design.

"Is everyone ready for the presentations?"

The guests responded with a resounding round of applause.

"First, I'd like to present to Sandy, the best office assistant in the world, a trip for two to Hawaii. Sandy, you have been there since I started the firm, and your tremendous help and expertise have been invaluable. I thank God for you."

"Thank you, boss. I have been trying to get there for thirty years."

"Yeah, I probably heard you mention it maybe once or twelve times. So, I thought I'd be of assistance. But, there is one condition. I want pictures. Next, I'd like to present bonuses to my partners, Celeste for a year and a half and James for about seven months. Celeste's bonus is five thousand dollars and James' bonus is twenty-five hundred."

"Oh thanks, Kyra. This will come in handy for the baby. Right, Tracy?"

"That's right, honey. Now I can get the nursery ready."

"Thanks, Kyra. I really appreciate this. I've been saving for the down payment on a house, and I think this will give me exactly what I need."

"No, problem Celeste. You've worked hard and you've earned it. You put in a lot of extra hours, and the firm wouldn't have made the great strides that it has without you. That goes for you too, James. Since you have come on board, we have done great things together. Now for our construction crews, both A and B; each person will receive a weekend getaway for two. But please, only use them when construction is not going on. Now that that's done, does anyone want dessert?"

"Well, actually I don't think we should stop the gift giving right now. Let's continue a little longer."

"I'm not sure I'm following you, Larkel."

"Well, I have a gift of my own. Kyra, we've spent almost everyday of the last six months together. We've had great adventures, we've worked closely on the designing and construction of my building, and we've been through a few ups and downs. It seems like a lot longer than six months. What I'm trying to say is I don't think I could imagine spending the rest of my life without you. Kyra, would you give me the pleasure of spending the rest of my life with you as your husband and you as my wife. I think we do far more than compliment each other. I know that throughout the time we have spent together..."

"Yes," Kyra almost screamed.

"Yes?"

"Yes, I'll marry you. You don't need to do a mini commercial. You had me on the word *would*." With that, Larkel slipped a ring on Kyra's finger.

"Show us the ring, Ky!" Sandy yelled as the tears ran down her face.

Can you believe it! I'm getting married. Wait until I tell Mom and Dad. They will be excited. They really like Lark. That's my pet name for him. He's so great. He's everything a girl could want in a husband. He's charming, considerate, kind, sexy, sweet, caring, strong, tender, gentle, secure, athletic.... I think you get the picture. We have to set a date. I'm sure it will be after the graduation and after the technology center is open.

Chapter Fourteen

No sooner than Kyra had made it in for the evening, her mind immediately went to work on trying to come up with the perfect time to schedule a wedding that fit both her and Larkel's schedules.

She couldn't help but constantly admire the beautiful ring Larkel had chosen for her. It was perfect. It was absolutely exquisite. The center stone was emerald cut and was surrounded by baguettes. The wide band had flat emerald cut diamonds craftily planted within the sides. Each diamond sparkled from each angle as she turned the ring.

Not able to make headway with a possible date or even a possible month for the wedding without discussing it with Larkel, Kyra decided to put everything out of her mind- at least for the moment.

She slowly shifted gears to working on her dissertation. She had made great headway on it in just a few short months. This type of progress was unheard of. Kyra had actually started gathering the data for her research during her last few courses. This allowed her to speed up the process of the compilation of the required five chapters. Now, it was time for her to apply the finishing touches.

When will be a good time for the wedding? Kyra thought not being able to stay focused on her homework. *Let me look at the calendar. Lark and I have so many things going on. His grand opening is scheduled to be held in two weeks. My graduation is two weeks after that. Then, I'm throwing Tracy's baby shower one week later. See what I mean? So, when will be a good time for a wedding? All of our family and friends are local, so we don't have to worry about people traveling into town. I guess Lark and I will need to sit down and decide how soon we want this wedding to take place or if we want a long engagement.*

Once again trying to channel her energy into her homework, Kyra vowed to focus on the task at hand. She needed to ensure the university did not reject her dissertation. And she absolutely did not want any last minute surprises. For the rest of the weekend, the dissertation was Kyra's priority.

But, on Monday, it was back to the office. Sitting at her desk wearing a crème cowl neck sweater with a pair of loose dark brown slacks, she was completely engrossed in her work. But with all the other life events on the horizon, Kyra's mind wandered from time to time.

"Sandy, can you come into my office please?"

"Sure boss. I'll be right in."

"Sandy, I know that this is not company business, but can you help with the arrangements for Larkel's grand opening?"

"Sure, I don't mind at all. What do you need me to do?"

"I've already made the arrangements with the caterers, but I need you to follow up with them. Then, I need you to call "We Decorate" in Ontario and discuss the color scheme with them, making sure that everything falls into place."

"What color scheme are you using?"

"Larkel wants royal blue and ivory."

"That's going to be really pretty, yet masculine."

"Then, I need to call his mother and his sisters to see if they want to put their hands in this. You know, I don't want to step on any toes."

"Well, you are going to be his wife, so I'm sure they'll understand."

"They have been pretty understanding, but you know how the women of the family can be when it comes to the men of the family. I just want to let them know that there's room for all of us."

"Larkel is really lucky to have you, Kyra."

"Thanks, Sandy. And thanks for your help. I really appreciate it."

Okay, now that the final arrangements for Lark's big day are set, I can move on to item number two, my graduation party. Tracy and Vanessa have volunteered to help with everything. This time my graduation party will be held at the Marriot. My sister-in-law Eyana is going to be in charge of the program. Everything is falling into place nicely. Let me call Nessa and see if she needs anything.

"Hey, Vanessa. What's up cousin?"

"Not much. I'm just running around with my head cut off trying to make sure that everything for you is in order."

"You know I appreciate you. Have you talked to Tracy today?"

"Yeah, as a matter of fact I'm about to pick her up, so we can check out the banquet hall for your party. We're going to draw up the seating chart and the floor arrangement, so we can have the DJ and the dance floor perfectly situated."

"That sounds good. Just make sure Tracy doesn't overdo it. You know she's in her eighth month."

"I know girl. She'll be okay. I just have to keep her from eating everything she sees."

"I know what you mean. She has gained so much weight. I told her she better lay off because all that weight is not the baby."

"Okay, well let me go. I'll call you from the hotel if we have any problems or questions. Don't worry girl; it's all coming together. Oh, one other thing. Your colors are purple and lime green right?"

"Purple and lime green! Girl!"

"I'm just playing. I know everything's supposed to be black."

"Vanessa, stop playing. When I get there on February 7, the only colors I want to see are silver, black, and white."

"Girl, like I said we got this." They both laughed as they disconnected the call.

She is so crazy. She has jokes for weeks. Between her and Tracy, I'm kept in stitches. What's next? Who is making all that noise?

Realizing the noise was coming from James' office, Kyra jumped up from her chair and nearly ran down the hall.

"Celeste, leave my office. We can't talk here. I told you that last night. This is not the time or the place."

"You think you can just brush me off, James? I don't think so. Who do you think you are?"

"Celeste! James! What is going on? What's the problem?"

"Nothing, Ky. I'll handle it. I just need to work out some things with Celeste."

"Does this have anything to do with the firm or is this personal?"

"It's personal, and it's really none of your business, Kyra. This is between me and James. And I want to talk to you now, James. You owe me an explanation."

"Time out! Celeste, you go into your office and let me talk to James."

"Kyra, I already told you that this is none of your business."

"Look, Celeste. I'm not asking you. I'm telling you. Go into your office. This may not be any of my business, but since you want to bring it to my place of business, I'm making it my business."

By this time, Sandy was standing inside the doorway with a bewildered look on her face. "Sandy, please take Celeste into her office, and see if you can get her to calm down. I'll talk to James," Kyra yelled.

"Come on, Celeste. I suggest you take Kyra's advice." Reluctantly, Celeste turned and walked out.

"Okay, James. I'm listening. What's going on?"

"Look, Ky. I made a bad decision, and I've already told Tracy about it. I got involved with Celeste. Nothing too serious, but still it was wrong. I know."

"What do you mean nothing too serious? What happened between the two of you?"

"Mostly flirtation and a little touching and some kissing here and there. She wanted to take things to the next level, but I decided not to. I don't know how I got mixed up in this. I love Tracy. I have for twelve years. I don't know where things went wrong."

"James, there has to more to it than what you are saying. A woman wouldn't just go off after a little flirting. Did the two of you have sex? Just tell me the truth, James, so I can know what's going on."

"Okay, Kyra. Listen. I didn't have sex with her. We were here one weekend, and things were getting really hot and heavy. We hadn't talked about how far we would go, but we were kissing and before I knew it, I had her on her desk. She began to unbutton my pants, and I let her. I guess she thought I was ready to go all the way, so she leaned back on the desk waiting for me to take her. And maybe I would have, but right then, my phone rang. My phone was right next to her on the desk, and Tracy's face appeared on the display. Celeste picked up my phone and was about to answer it. At the moment, I realized what I was doing. And I realized she didn't care who we could possibly be hurting. I grabbed my phone and ran out of there. Every since then, I have been avoiding her. She is out of control. I confessed everything to Tracy last night."

"How is Tracy dealing with all of this?"

"She almost went into premature labor after I told her."

"Oh, James. Why didn't you tell me? You and Tracy are family."

At that moment, Celeste came running back into James' office with a shiny object in her hand.

"Celeste, what are you doing? Have you lost your mind?" Kyra screamed as she moved towards Celeste.

"Hey, Celeste! What the hell?" James said in alarm.

"Sandy, call the police! Celeste! Stop! No, James. Don't touch her. The last thing we need is for her to press charges against you," Kyra yelled as she restrained Celeste and took the object from her hand.

"I'm sorry, Kyra. She wouldn't stay in her office."

"It's okay, Sandy. Are the police on their way?"

"Yes, they're coming now."

"James, just stay in your office," Kyra instructed.

Talk about drama. I cannot believe this. That's the last straw. That girl has got to go. This is absolute grounds for termination. She could really hurt the firm's reputation. I hate to do it, but she brought this on herself. Crazy heifer. Wait until Tracy hears about this. This could really take her into labor.

"Kyra, the police are here, but Celeste left."

"Ask them to come into my office and ask James to come in. I want to file a report."

"Good afternoon, ma'am. I'm Detective Johnson, and this is my partner Detective Williams. I understand there was some type of disturbance here. Would you like to file a report?"

"As a matter of fact I would. Let me give you the details as I know them. Please, have a seat."

Kyra proceeded to tell them about the disturbance and how Celeste had basically tried to attack James with a letter opener.

Chapter Fifteen

By the end of the week, Kyra felt as though everything was closing in on her. She was now back to having only one partner, and new clients had come to the firm requesting their services. She wasn't sure if she and James could handle everything in a timely manner with him and his wife expecting their first child, her own graduation, and all else life had to offer.

But she was determined to make a go of it. Trying to remain proactive, she drove to her cousin Vanessa's home, so they could go shopping for Larkell's grand opening. After a few minutes inside, Kyra had already grown anxious and was ready to get on with it.

"Nessa, are you ready to go shopping? I thought you would be ready when I got here."

"Let me put some shoes on. What type of outfit are you looking for?"

"I don't know for sure. But, I'm sure something will catch my eye."

"Okay, let's get this shopping frenzy on the road. His opening is a dressy affair right?"

"Right."

"Okay, I just want to be on the lookout for the right type of outfit. So, Ky you had started telling me about the office drama. What happened?"

"Let's stop at Dairy Queen, so I can get a Strawberry Cheesequake before I begin my story."

"You mean cheesecake?"

"No, they call it cheesequake. It is so delicious."

After picking up a few tasty treats from Dairy Queen, the ladies proceeded to the mall.

"Alright Nordstrom's, here we come. Now stop stalling, Ky. Give me the scoop."

"Okay, here is the scoop. After I finished talking to you the other day, I heard some yelling and screaming coming from down the hall. I got up and ran down to James' office. Celeste was standing in his doorway yelling and screaming about how he did her wrong and how she wants to talk and he's going to pay."

"Pay for what?"

"I didn't know at the time. All I know is she was going off. Then, I asked Sandy to take Celeste into her office, and Celeste had the nerve to tell me that it was none of my business."

"How did she make that mistake? I know you had something to say about that."

"I wanted to knock the hell out of her. I had been waiting for this day ever since they started acting suspicious. I needed this to happen, so I could get her out of my face. I can't say she's totally at fault. James played his role too. But see what she did wrong was to bring that mess into the office. She should have kept her private drama private. But no, she wanted to act like a jealous teenager out on the high school yard."

"So, what happened after she went to her office?"

"I went in to talk to James to see why hell was breaking loose at the office. He gave me his side of the story."

"Which is what? He's been trying to get a little on the side?"

"According to him, he didn't actually take any. He decided to dabble a little bit."

"Yeah right. That girl didn't go off for nothing."

"Well, Vanessa I don't know. I'm just telling you what he told me. But while we were talking, Celeste came in with her letter opener and tried to stab James."

"Oh my goodness. Did anyone get hurt?"

"Thankfully, no."

"What was she thinking?"

"The hell if I know. I had to grab her and restrain her to get her out of the office. Then, she tried to go loco on me. I wanted to slap the hell out of her, but she would have tried to file a lawsuit against me. So, anyway after that, Sandy called the police. They came, and I filed a report."

"So, what happens now?"

"I called her to come clear out her office."

"Are you serious? You're just going to let her go?"

"Heck yeah. You don't know all the scandals that she can cause. She has been involved with client after client and contractor after contractor. I don't need any more drama. If she can't draw the line between her personal and private life, then I need to."

"Yeah, you're right. I understand."

While sharing the story of the office drama, Kyra and Vanessa tried on outfit after outfit, until Kyra found exactly what she thought would help set the atmosphere and until Vanessa found something she thought she couldn't live without.

"Let's pay for these clothes and get out of here. I need to meet with Lark. We need to talk about wedding plans tonight."

"So, you guys are going to set the date?"

"Hopefully. I'm anxious to get started on the planning just as soon as the grand opening, the graduation and my niece's birth have all passed."

"That's right. Tracy did say she's having a girl. You guys are going to be busy for the next couple of months."

"Tell me about it. But, all of the events are memorable events. I'm looking forward to all of them. Aren't you?"

"Girl, you know I'll be there every step of the way."

A few hours later, Kyra arrived home very exhausted from her day. *Let me put this stuff away, take a shower and find something to put on. Larkel should be pulling up in about half an hour. I really don't feel like dining in a restaurant tonight. Maybe we will just stay in and watch tv or put a movie on. I hope Larkel didn't make any big plans. After a day full of teaching classes and doing interviews, he's probably tired himself. What I really want to do is talk about us. I think I hear him coming up now.*

Kyra opened the door when she heard Lark step up to the porch. To her surprise, she opened the door to a large bouquet of flowers. As soon as she smelled their sweet fragrance, she immediately felt calm in her spirit.

"Hey, honey. It's good to see you. Thank you for the beautiful flowers. They smell heavenly. Um, and so do you," Kyra said as she got a whiff of his cologne as he moved into her face.

"Hi, baby. Come here. I haven't seen you in a couple of days."

"I know and that's much too long. Can we stay in tonight?"

"Absolutely. You must be reading my mind. I'm a little tired from so much busy work."

"Come over here and relax. Is there something you want me to get you?"

"Not right now. I just want you next to me."

"Good because I'm not going anywhere. But, can we discuss setting a date for the wedding?"

"You must be reading my mind again. I was going to ask you the exact same question. Do you want a long engagement or a short one?"

"To put it simply and plainly, a short one. What about you?"

"I would like a short engagement. I'm looking forward to totally putting our lives together. So, how short is short for you?"

"Well, I was going over our calendars, and I noticed that the last major event that needs to occur is Tracy's baby shower and, of course, the birth of the baby."

"What day is the baby due?"

"March 26."

"How long after the baby is born do you want to wait?"

"How about the next day? No seriously, how about April or May?"

"How about April? I'll have time off for spring break. What about you? Will you be able to get away from the office?"

"I don't foresee any problems with that at the moment. Things will be a little tight with only James and me working with the clients. But what about the technology center? You will have only been opened for a couple of months. Do you expect things to be in full throttle by then?"

"Hopefully, they will be. I have been accepting applications for students and staff for the last month. The center should be able to survive without me while I take my beautiful bride on a honeymoon."

"Okay, honey. Sounds like everything is coming together. Where is the calendar? We need to choose a specific Saturday."

"It should be the Saturday before Easter. I will either be off a week before or after Easter."

"Okay, that makes it April 10."

Chapter Sixteen

On Monday, it was back to the grind in the office.

"Good morning, Sandy."

"Good morning, Kyra. You have company in your office."

"Am I late for an appointment?"

"Not unless you were planning to meet with Celeste."

"What is she doing here?" Kyra asked in almost a whisper.

"I guess she wants to talk. I really didn't ask for any details."

Not knowing what to expect, Kyra walked cautiously into her office a little on guard. "Good morning, Celeste."

"Good morning, Kyra. I'm sorry for dropping in without an appointment. I just came by to collect my things and to apologize to you. You have never treated me unfairly since I've been here. I apologize for my actions. I should have handled myself a lot better than I did. I should have kept my private life separate from my professional life."

"Well, I'm glad you understand my position. I really don't believe I have another choice."

"If it's okay with you I'll clean out my office now."

"That's fine. I will have your final check ready at the end of the week. I'll have Sandy give you a call."

Lark's grand opening is this weekend. That means that I better get a move on with the plans for the Wheaton and the Pearce projects. I'm not accustomed to doing business deals with women. A husband and wife team, yes. But a woman as a sole proprietor, no. On both of these projects, Angela and Sheila can't seem to make up their minds if they want Spanish marble or Australian tile in the bathrooms. They don't know if they should have hardwood floors or not. They keep changing their minds about brick walls or dry walls with wallpaper. To top it off, they can't decide if they want the front of their twin beauty salon and spa to face the street or have an exclusive entrance. The good thing about working with them is that they are friends and they tend to think alike, although I think Angela is really running the show. When one of them changes her mind, the other falls in line. So, at least I don't have to deal with them yelling at each other and making my job any harder than it is.

The plans for the beauty salon, which is Angela's baby, are complete. She just needs to decide which materials she wants to use. The spa designs, on the other hand, are in limbo. Sheila can't decide how many saunas to put in, how many hot tubs, Jacuzzi's, swimming pools, etc. Maybe she will have made her final decisions by the next time we meet. Then, maybe I can finalize the drafts. Talk about needing closure.

"Kyra, your sister-in-law is here. Should I direct her to your office or one of the conference rooms?"

"Send her into my office. Thanks, Sandy."

"Good afternoon, Ky."

"Hey, Yani. Come on in. You are looking as beautiful as ever."

"Are you sure this is a good time? You look swamped."

"No, right now is actually an excellent time. I need a reprieve from the Wheaton and Pearce projects. I feel like I'm backed against a wall."

"What's the problem? Did someone overextend their credit and can't afford the job?"

"No, these women have more than enough money I'm sure. That's probably why they can afford to change their minds a hundred times about the designs and materials for their beauty salon and health spa. I'll just be glad when they make some final decisions. But enough about that. Let's talk about the graduation party."

"Okay. I've been working on the program and the menu. Vanessa and Tracy are doing the decorations and the hotel arrangements, right?"

"Yes, they have everything set in those categories. What do you have so far?"

"Well, I have all the entertainment worked out and I have a space for "open mike," so anyone who wants to say something can."

"That's fine. Whatever you think will be best. Just make sure you leave me a spot, so I can thank everyone for their love and support over the years."

"Girl, I hope you don't cry. Because if you cry, I'm going to cry."

"Girl, you will probably cry anyway. You don't have to wait for me."

"Funny, Ky. Real funny. Okay, girl. I just wanted to stop by and run these plans by you. I'll let you get back to your draft drama."

"Why are you in a hurry? I don't have anything pressing right now. I can't move forward on the Pearce Project until I meet with Sheila in the morning."

"What do you want to do?"

"I need to go to the mall and pick up Lark's gift for his grand opening."

"What are you getting him?"

"You'll just have to wait and see."

"Oh, so it's like that?"
"Yeah, it's like that."

Chapter Seventeen

Early Saturday morning, after taking an early morning jog, Kyra returned home to find Larkel still asleep. After a late dinner and driving Kyra home, they decided it was best he stay over instead of going home late and coming back early.

"Honey, wake up."

"Why? What time is it?"

"Time for you to head to the barber shop. Remember, you have an appointment for a fresh shave."

"Did you tell Jason that I need my head and my face shaved?"

"I called Jason, but he's out of town. I made you an appointment with Lavar. He knows the drill."

"How much time do I have until I need to be there?"

"About forty-five minutes. So, come on. Get into the shower."

"What are your plans for this morning?"

"I have an appointment this morning, too. You don't think I'm going to the grand opening like this do you?"

"Baby, you always look good."

"Thanks, but enough of the sweet talk. We need to hurry. I made your breakfast too. It's in the microwave. Make sure you eat before you go."

"Thanks, honey. What time do we need to meet back here?"

"At one or two. I need to go by the tailors and pick up your suit after I get my hair done."

"Okay, sweetie. I'll see you later."

Men. What would they do without us? The same thing we would do without them, nothing. I hope I don't have to sit all day in the beauty salon. I want to get in and get out. That's funny. Who do I know that has ever gone into a beauty salon and come right out? Well, I will have a good book with me. That should help the time move faster.

While waiting under the dryer at the hair salon, thoughts of the upcoming night filled Kyra's mind.

I hope Lark likes his gift. I really didn't know what to get him. But I think this is appropriate. If I think it was hard to shop for him for this occasion, just wait for the wedding. Oh, the wedding! We have about three good months to plan. We haven't chosen a location. We better get moving. Maybe I should be looking at bridal magazines while I'm getting my hair done instead of reading this book.

With her hair beautifully styled, Kyra was ready to run errands and continue on with her day. Her next stop was the tailors and back to the house. *I wonder if Lark is excited as I am about his accomplishment. I don't think he really wanted a party, but I think deep down he's really excited. He's just so laid back that sometimes it's hard to tell. Looks like he made it back before me. I wonder what he's up to.*

"Lark? I'm home. Honey? Where are you?"

"I was on the phone."

"Oh. Who was that?"

"That was Tracy. She said she was having false labor pains, and she doesn't know if she and James will be able to make it tonight."

"I hope she's okay. Did she sound worried or stressed? I better call her back."

Getting her best friend back on the phone, Kyra went into protective mode, "Tracy, what's wrong?"

"It's nothing to get alarmed about, Ky. I thought I was going into premature labor, so I went to the emergency room. But they said it was false labor. James said maybe I should just stay off my feet."

"Is everything okay, Trace? Is everything with you and James okay?"

"Everything has been a lot better around here. It's almost like he's back to his old self except better. He's been so attentive, and he's been really helping out more around here."

"So, no more disappearing acts?"

"No, he's here all the time."

"Good. If you need anything, don't hesitate to call."

"Thanks, Ky. We'll try to make it, but if you don't see us tell Larkel we said, 'Congratulations, and we will get together soon.'"

"Okay, sweetie. You get some rest and be careful with my niece."

After relaxing for only a short moment, Kyra dozed off in her Lazy-Boy recliner for about thirty minutes. Touching her gently, Larkel aroused her from her sleep.

"Baby, it's almost time to go. I just showered before you came in so it's all yours. Where did you put my suit?"

"It's in the hall closet. I'll be ready in half an hour."

Just over an hour later, they pulled up to the tech center.

"Wow, look at all these cars. Who are all these people?"

"Remember, the grand opening is open to the public, so there's no telling who's all here in addition to your friends, family, and colleagues."

"You invited my colleagues?"

"Absolutely. Don't you know how many people you have in your corner? Oh, look there's a good spot to park. Right in front of the door."

"I wonder why no one got this spot. What does that sign say? When did that get here? I didn't see it yesterday."

"Why don't you get out and take a closer look."

"Ky, what have you done? This is awesome. My own parking spot."

"Honey, don't you think it's right to be able to pull up to your own business and be able to park without driving around like a lost puppy?"

"This is absolutely the best. Thanks, Kyra."

"You are quite welcome. I think we better go in before everyone begins to think the party is out here."

As the couple walked in the door, shouts rang out!

"The man of the hour has arrived. Everybody on three. 1, 2, 3. For he's a jolly good fellow, for he's a jolly good fellow........"

"Thanks, everyone. I appreciate you taking your time out to come and celebrate this day with me. It was a long time coming. I can't believe I'm finally here. And I couldn't have done it without my fiancée Kyra. Didn't she do a wonderful job on the design of this building?" More cheers and shouts rang out.

"Honey, why don't you take them on the grand tour, and then we will all go into the conference room for dinner. I'll go check to make sure everything is on order."

"Sounds great. We will meet you there in about a half hour or so."

After making her way to the conference room, Kyra sees Larkel's mother and moves in her direction.

"Mrs. Sherten, thank you for working with Sandy to oversee the dinner and make sure the caterers had access to everything they needed. The room is absolutely beautiful. You would think it was an actual banquet room rather than a conference room."

"Kyra, I don't mind helping out at all. And you must stop calling me Mrs. Sherten. You can call me Mom. You are already part of the family."

"Thank you for making me feel welcome."

After taking a closer look at the decorations and quickly surveying the food, Kyra went back to the car to get the gift she had concealed in Lark's trunk.

"I think I hear everyone making their way here," Kyra announced. "Vanessa, can you take Larkel and his mom and sisters to the head table?"

"Sure, Ky. No problem."

"May I have everyone's attention please? The servers are ready to serve dinner, so please find a table anywhere in the room and have a seat. There are tables reserved for family members; just look for the signs. After dinner is served and eaten, we will invite those of you who want to present gifts or kind words to come up to the podium. Enjoy your meal."

Having these types of functions really take a lot out of you. But, they really are worth every drop of sweat. From what Larkel shared about himself, his mother and father both worked hard in order to provide for their children. They were able to go to private schools, grow up in a suburban neighborhood, and attend the college of their choice. Along with providing the best opportunities for their children, the Shertens also taught them about morals, ethics and respect. Larkel is always courteous and respectful to everyone who comes in contact with him. Even when people are rude to him, he finds a way to smooth out the situation with a smile. That is really a rarity in the society we live in today. Today, people are out for themselves and whatever they can get. They will step all over you to get to the top rung of the ladder. But not Larkel. He went through all the legal procedures to attain all that he has accomplished.

I am so proud of his accomplishments. Some teachers only do what they think they are paid to do. Larkel gives and teaches with his whole heart. I have seen him reach out time and time again to his students, providing them with additional conference and office hours when necessary. Because of his dedication to his students and his profession, he has decided to open this school and focus on the underprivileged. Although the center will be open to everyone, his focus is on securing federal grants that will pay the students' tuition.

Well, I guess anyone would be able to tell that I am proud of my fiancé. It's time to get this show on the road.

Approaching the podium once again, Kyra addressed the guests, "Once again, may I have your attention, please. I know that many of you have a gift that you would like to present or words that you would like to share. If you could please begin to form a line to the side of the podium and along the wall, we can get started. I would like to offer the opportunity to Larkel's mother to go first."

"Larkel, son, I just want you to know that with each growing endeavor that you pursue, you make me more and more proud. I don't believe that there is a mother on earth who is as proud as I am. And if your father were alive today, I'm sure he would concur. You know, being his only son, you were the apple of his eye. Tonight, I would like to present to you, my son, Larkel Renald Sherten this plaque of appreciation."

After Larkel's mother's presentation, Kyra's mother was next in line to present.

"To Larkel, my future son-in-law, I am proud to stand here today in honor of you and say that you are a fine young man, and you will definitely do this community a lot of good. They should be proud to have you. As I have watched you over the past several months, I must say that my admiration for you continues to grow. We live in a time where young people seem to be losing hope more and more each day. Thankfully, we have people like you that have a desire to continue to uplift them and show them that all is not lost. Keep up the good work, Larkel. And if you ever need a helping hand, please don't hesitate to call. I always have time to spend on a good cause. My husband and I, we present to you these engraved name plates for your office door and for your desk."

Next, a gentleman near Larkel's age approached the podium.

"Larkel, my friend and my colleague, my congrats to you on accomplishing your dream. I know this may be hard to believe, but I really admire you, and I say that will all due respect. We grew up together, played football together, went to college together, and in the midst of it all, we have shared good times and not so good times. Through it all, you have always been a person of integrity, someone that I could count on. I wish you the best and pray for your continued success and the success of your technology center. In closing, I would like to present to you and your organization a $10,000 check to be added to the scholarship fund. I know it will be put to good use."

After each person who wanted to share expressions of love had shared, Kyra once again graced the podium.

"I would like to add to the many wonderful comments that have already gone forth. I am very proud to stand here, not only as the woman who loves and respects you dearly, but as a member of this community, and say congratulations to you Larkel for your accomplishments and for striving to continue to see your dream through all the various stages that you have gone through to get to this point. I just want to encourage you to continue to have the dedication, determination, and desire that you have because that is what it is going to take in order for everything to continue to soar to the heights of excellence that you desire for yourself, our youth and the vision that you have for this company. As you continue to pour out so much of yourself into others, I want you to be forever mindful of who you are and what you represent. In doing that, you will always continue to be an example of an individual who has something to offer to those you come in contact with. My gift for you tonight is a 16X20 picture of yourself that will be posted in the entry foyer. The bottom of the frame is engraved. It states your name and position as founder of this fine technology center."

Closing out her segment, Kyra once again opened the mike up to the floor to anyone who wanted to share congrats to Larkel. From the back of the room, a tall, slender woman rose from her seat and said, "I would like to share." As she walked to the podium, all eyes were on her and the beautiful red evening gown she was wearing. The red of the gown radiated and the silver sequins sparkled like a million dollars.

The woman began with an introduction:

"Good evening, everyone. My name is Lauren Sanders, and I have a special presentation for Lar. Oh, I'm sorry. That was my pet name for him some years ago. Larkel, it is so wonderful to see your dream become a reality. I know you have wanted this for some time now." As she spoke with her eyes looking directly into his, she seemed to ignore everyone else in the room, including Kyra. Before presenting her gift of $25,000, she asked Larkel to come up to the podium. With her heels, she matched his height perfectly. As she handed him the check, she leaned in and kissed him squarely on the lips. Standing there not knowing what to say, Larkel watched her walk out the door. Coming back to his senses, he began to speak.

"I want to thank each and every one of you who added this magnanimous event into your schedules. I will be forever thankful for sharing this event with each of you. I would like to give a special thanks to my fiancée Kyra, my mother and my sisters for putting this special event together. They really know how to throw a celebration, don't they? Thank you for all the words of praise and encouragement and for all the wonderful gifts. But the night is still young, so everybody make your way over to the desert bar and fill your stomachs. And if you wouldn't mind, the photographer is here, and I would like to have pictures taken of everyone."

Eyana and Vanessa couldn't take their eyes off Kyra. They were watching for her reaction to the sudden appearance and disappearance of the woman in the red dress. As soon as they were able to get Kyra alone, the questions began to flow.

When Kyra went to the ladies' room feeling sick to her stomach, Yani and Nessa followed.

"Kyra, are you okay?" Nessa queried.

"You don't look so good," Yani interjected.

"Who was that?" Nessa wanted to know.

"Look ladies, I don't know, but I will get to the bottom of this. Believe me. For now, let's just enjoy the evening. Too many thoughts are already running through my mind and reminding me of Marcus. Let's go back out there and grin and bear it."

Eyana and Vanessa looked at each other and followed Kyra back into the conference room.

They didn't know what to make of it, but they followed her lead.

Chapter Eighteen

That night, when Kyra and Larkel made it back to her home, Kyra still had her mind on Lauren. After the experience, Kyra felt something unlock within her. As she undressed, she felt a desire for Larkel that took her by surprise. After all they had experienced together and all the moments of touching and caressing they had shared, Kyra had something holding her back from full intimacy, even though on a few occasions they had slept in the same bed.

After removing every single item of clothing she was wearing, Kyra walked over to Larkel who was sitting on the side of the bed. When he saw her approaching him completely nude, he understood their relationship was moving to the next level. He watched her slowly walk toward him. He admired every inch of her body, but he couldn't help to notice the look of desire in her eyes.

He attempted to stand to meet her as she reached his side of the bed, but Kyra placed her hand on his shoulder. He understood that to mean 'sit still.'

Slowly, Kyra placed one leg on each side of Larkel's legs and pushed the upper part of her body against his, causing him to lie back on the bed. Embracing her around her waist, Larkel immediately took charge as he gently turned her over onto her back. The entire time, they shared deep kisses and never stopped gazing into each other's eyes.

Slowly, Larkel moved into the depths of Kyra as she received him willingly.

Chapter Nineteen

The next morning, still wrapped around each other, Larkel whispered, "Baby, I just want to thank you for throwing the grand opening party. It is definitely something I will not forget."

"You deserve it. I hope it was everything you wanted."

"It was more than I could have dreamed of, and the gifts were spectacular. They will add something special to the building, giving it a personal touch."

"We must have all had that in mind when we decided what gift to give you."

"Let me ask you something though. Did you and my family discuss the gifts? They all seemed to be in synch."

"Now, do you really need to know all the details?"

"Not really. But, thank you, again. What do you want to do today?"

"Well, before I decide anything, I have a question for you," Kyra said slowly as she sat up and turned toward Larkel, while looking down at her hands. She didn't really know how to approach the subject or how Lark would take the inquisition, but she didn't believe in beating around the bush or holding back.

Larkel gently placed his hand underneath her chin and lifted her face up. "You can ask me anything," he said softly as he noticed her hesitation.

"Ok," Kyra responded with a hint of hesitation.

"Go ahead, sweetie," Lark encouraged.

"Who is the woman who was wearing the red dress?" Kyra blurted out.

"She is my ex."

"Ex what? Ex-wife or ex-girlfriend?"

"Ex-girlfriend. We stopped dating a little over a year ago. I haven't spoken to her or seen her for about nine months."

"How did she know about the grand opening?"

"I don't know. But let me say this- things are over between us. They have been for some time. You don't need to worry about her, or anyone else for that matter," Lark said feeling Kyra's vibes.

"What concerns me is the fact that she walked in and kissed you on the lips as if it was the thing to do. That is not something I view as acceptable."

"I certainly understand. I didn't see that coming, but I assure you it will not happen again. Kyra Fraser, let me explain something to you about me just in case you don't have a clear picture yet. I am a one-woman man. I do not have time nor do I particularly enjoy seeing more than one woman at a time. I have had plenty of opportunities to do so, but I give my woman the same respect I expect to receive. I wouldn't want her sharing her time with another man, so I'm not going to do it to her. I believe a strong relationship is built on trust, honesty, integrity, and love. That is what I am bringing to our relationship and nothing less. And, I apologize for Lauren's inappropriate actions."

After Lark's verbal presentation of love, all Ky could do was slowly move over next to him, place her arms around his neck and begin to kiss him softly and deeply, allowing him to feel her passion and love. Just as soon as he could fully reciprocate, the phone rang. Kyra slowly pulled away after the third ring. She saw 'James' on the caller ID.

"Hello?"

"Ky, are you busy? It's about Tracy."

"What's wrong with her James?"

"She went into labor. It's the real thing this time. We're at the hospital. Can you come down?"

"Of course, I'll be right there."

"Thanks, Ky. I'll let her know."

"What's wrong? Did Tracy go into labor?" Larkel asked.

"Yes, I need to get over there right away."

"Do you want me to go with you?"

"That's up to you. I know you're tired and this could take a while."

"You're tired, too. Let's get dressed, and I'll start the car."

"Thanks, honey. Give me three minutes."

I am going to have a serious talk with my newborn niece just as soon as she is old enough to understand about love and romance. She chose the most inopportune time to be born. She better not take all day either, or I will have something to say about that too. Who am I kidding? I have been looking forward to this day since Trace told me she was pregnant. I'm going to be an auntie again. I am going to spoil this baby rotten. Watch out world, Auntie is on her way.

Upon Larkel and Kyra's arrival at the maternity ward, they immediately make their way to Tracy's room. "Tracy, we're here sweetie. How are you feeling?"

"I'm ready to have this baby. I'm dilated to four centimeters."

"Did the doctor say why you went into labor so early?"

"No, not yet. They're thinking that there was a miscalculation on the due date. The baby is fine;

she's not in any danger. They kept telling me that she seemed big for the dates that I gave them, so maybe that's why she's coming now. Oh, my God! Ky, get the nurse."

"Hey, we need help in here! She's having strong pains."

"Excuse me, Miss. I need both of you to leave the room. We need to transport her to delivery; the baby is crowning. Where is Mr. Talbert?"

"He's in the hallway. Lark, can you get him? I'll see you when you come out, Trace."

"No, I want you to come in with James."

Oh my goodness. I don't know if I can handle this. Lord, give me strength, Kyra thought.

Once in the delivery room, James began to immediately coach Tracy.

"Come on, Tracy. You can do it. Just breathe girl, breathe."

After only thirty more minutes of labor, the baby's head was out of the birth canal. Soon, the rest of the body followed, and Tracy was able to lay back and relax.

Oh, she's beautiful. She looks just like Tracy, but she has James' nose. She is absolutely adorable.

"Mr. Talbert, would you like the honor of cutting the umbilical chord?" the attending doctor asked.

"I guess so. Okay, here goes."

After the nurse took the baby to be cleaned, Kyra asked, "What's her name going to be?"

"We decided on Jasmeen Trashawn Talbert," James answered.

"That is absolutely beautiful. I can call her Jazz. Let me go and tell Lark the news. I'll see you after they finishing cleaning the baby and take you to your room."

Motherhood has to be the most wonderful thing on the face of this earth. I wonder how many children Lark and I will have once we get married. I wonder what our children will look like. Thank God that male-pattern baldness comes from the mother, so I don't have to worry about our children loosing their hair at an early age like Lark did. That's why he wears his head clean-shaven. But, Lavar at Whip Appeal keeps him looking good.

Children shouldn't be an issue for us because we have finished all the schooling that we desire to have and our businesses are off the ground and well under way. Money is no problem, so we have nothing standing on our way. We're both ready. Thirty years is long enough to wait to have a child. Let's get this show on the road.

Chapter Twenty

After receiving an urgent call from the university on Monday morning, Kyra rushed right over to the campus.

I wonder what is going on at the dean's office. They left me an urgent message saying I need to come down to the university right away. I hope there isn't a problem with my dissertation. It took me about a year to compose the whole thing and compose draft after draft. I do not wish to travel down those roads again. I just want to get my dissertation signed off, so I can celebrate my graduation, Kyra thought as she made her way to the dean's office.

"Good morning is Dean Henderson in?"

"Yes, he is. Do you have an appointment?"

"No, my name is Kyra Fraser and a message was left this morning by your office saying that it was urgent that I come in."

"Oh, that's right. I left that message. I'll let the dean know that you are here."

I hope this doesn't take long. I need to get to the office and meet with Sheila to finalize the details on her health spa. Then, I want to go visit Tracy and Jasmeen. I wonder if Tracy will still want to have the baby shower. Let's see, Jasmeen will be three weeks old by then. We can still have the baby shower. The only difference will be that the baby will be present.

"Ms. Fraser, the dean will see you now."

"Good morning, Dean Henderson. I received a message that you needed to see me right away. Is there a problem with my dissertation?"

"No, the problem is with your residency hours. We only have documentation for five of your peer days. Have you completed all ten?"

"Yes. I did all ten within the first year of the program. Which five do you have documentation for?"

"This is the documentation that we have. Look through it and determine what's missing."

"That wasn't difficult. The documentation for the five days that I spent in Canada is missing."

"You completed five consecutive peer days?"

"Yes."

"And were they approved by your core?"

"Yes, they were as were the evaluations."

"Well, all we need is a copy of those evaluations for your file. Your dissertation has already been approved. We just needed to make sure that all other requirements were completed. I don't know how we missed the documents. While you are here, you can look through the final copy of your dissertation before it is sent to be bound. Just stop by the secretary's desk, and she will assist you. And as soon as you have those documents ready, fax them into my office."

"Thank you, Dean Henderson."

Well that was easy. They almost scared me to death. Talk about having your stress level go through the roof. I need to go home and locate those documents on the Canada peer days and fax them over to the dean's office. I don't want to give them any excuses for not allowing me to graduate. I am so out of there.

I don't understand why my advisor did not forward a copy of those documents. Those were probably the most informative of the peer days. Not only did we share information that was useful, informative, and interesting, but we also were able to allot some time to enjoying the beautiful scenery of Victoria, Canada. We visited Butchart Gardens, did a little traversing through the mountainous area, and were able to enjoy fine cuisine every evening. Our hosts, the McGuigans, even invited us to dinner one night at their home. That was a lovely treat, a welcome change to restaurant dining.

Going immediately back home, Kyra went into her office and began to tear the place apart. *Let's see. Where are those documents? I'm sure I have a flash drive with all the peer day evaluations saved on it. Here it is. Okay, step one done. I'll just take this to the office with me and fax it from there. I have just over an hour to get to the office before my appointment with Sheila. That means I have time to grab a bite to eat. A salad sounds good.*

After enjoying a fresh grilled chicken salad, Kyra drove to the firm and immediately went into her office. Ten minutes later, Sandy buzzed her private line. "Kyra, Ms. Pearce has arrived for her two o'clock appointment."

"Sandy, please seat her in my drafting room, please."

Quickly moving down the hall, Kyra stepped in to meet her client. "Good afternoon, Sheila. How are you?"

"Just fine. And you?"

"I have no complaints. But I do have a few questions for you though. Are you ready to get started?"

"Absolutely. I am looking forward to moving this project towards completion."

"My sentiments exactly. Okay, let's start by working on the exterior of the building. You need to decide how much lighting will come from outside versus the interior lighting. Then, you need to focus on how the different amenities will be arranged inside because that will have a direct bearing on the outside design. Once we have accomplished those tasks, then we can decide the appropriate flooring for each room. I can show you samples of other very nicely done spas. Maybe these pictures will help you to reach your decision. While you are looking through those pictures, is there something that I can offer you to drink? We have hot and cold beverages available."

"I would like a cup of coffee, if you don't mind. That might get my brain moving."

"Sandy, can you bring in a cup of coffee for Ms. Pearce."

I hope this is the last day that I have to deal with indecisiveness. I am ready to move this project on to James, so he can consult the construction crew. I pray that after being in the planning stage for an extended period of time, we can now move through the next few stages rapidly. Thankfully, Angela has moved into the construction stage with her beauty salon. Maybe that will be incentive enough to get Sheila there with her. I'm sure because they are opening conjoined shops, they will want to be ready to open at the same time. That will enable them to have a grand, grand opening. That will be a spectacular event. We really do need an upscale health spa in the Inland Empire. And one that has a hair salon attached to it is even better.

Chapter Twenty-One

Well, graduation is in two days. This last week has been eventful. Everyone is progressing in his/her personal adventure. Tracy and Jasmeen are doing fine, and James is walking around like the proud father. He can barely contain his joy. He walks around like a Cheshire cat. He seems as though he has some newfound energy. I've always known him to be energetic, but this is different. He is really staying on top of the construction crews to work diligently and expediently. I'm glad to see him and Tracy happy again. They have been together for a long time, and they deserve every bit of happiness that comes their way.

Larkel's tech center is doing far better than he could have ever imagined in this short period of time. All of the computer stations are filled on a daily basis. Classes are being held, and the programs are coming together. He even had two more positive responses to his grant proposals this past week, thanks to his grant writers. However, there is a down side to all of the excitement: It leaves him extremely exhausted. Sometimes, he doesn't have enough energy to teach his classes at UCR. Kyra has been trying to get him to let his staff have more responsibilities, but he insists that they are just not ready yet. He's going to have to make some decisions. He doesn't want any of his students to lack because of his inability to measure up to his own standards due to fatigue, so he's either going to have to resign from UCR or delegate more responsibility to his staff at the center.

As for the firm, everything is moving along smoothly. The Wheaton and Pearce projects are finally in the construction phases. Their grand openings have been scheduled to occur in four months. Sandy is doing double duty. Not only is she doing her nine-to-five job here and keeping things in order, she is helping Kyra's mom fill in the details of the wedding. She is such a great asset.

I wonder what's going on with Celeste. I haven't heard from or seen her since she came to pick up her final check. I really want to invite her to my graduation party and to my wedding, but for obvious reasons I can't. I wouldn't want to be the one to stir up any drama. Too bad things turned out this way. Well, I guess some friendships come and some go.

So, as you can see, everything is moving along nicely. Every day that I awake, I have butterflies in my stomach. Graduation is almost here. I can't wait. Oh, that reminds me. I need to call Vanessa to see if all the final arrangements have been made for the celebration. Money is not an issue, because Lark paid for everything. Wasn't that sweet of him? I need to call Eyana to see if her butterflies have calmed down. She's so worried she will make a mistake and disappoint me. Who am I, the perfectionist of the year? I just want us to have a good time and enjoy ourselves as we celebrate an accomplishment. And finally, I need to call Tracy to check on my niece and see if they need anything while James is out on the construction site. Then, when all the calls have been made, I will meet Larkel later for dinner. I hope he's not too exhausted. I'm really looking forward to seeing him. I haven't seen him since Monday when I stopped by the center.

Chapter Twenty-Two

Today is the day! Today is the day! I wish my grandmother were here to enjoy this with me. But, I am grateful that my mother, father, and brothers are here to help me celebrate. They are so proud of me. But, I don't think they know that they are my strength. I have accomplished everything with their love and support. I wonder if they are all out there. I've been breaking my neck to try to look into the crowds, but there are so many loved ones in the crowd that it is hard to see. Maybe I can send a text message to Lark. He said he was going to save a space for everyone. I already know that

Tracy, James, Jasmeen, Eyana, Rod, Khalil, Vanessa, and Sandy are here. I saw them in the parking lot.

Great! Lark says that they are here, my mom, my dad, Noah, August, Mrs. Sherten, and my two sister-in-laws. Now I can relax. Ha! That's funny! I don't think I'm going to relax until I cross the stage. Oh, they're calling us now. Here, I go.

"Next, we present the Ph.D.'s from the department of Fine Arts, Drafting, and Design. Please come forward."

"Dr. DeJon Alexander."

"Dr. Dejore Clifton."

"Dr. Randi Danford."

"Dr. Justin Dryser."

"Dr. Nicholas Evergreen."

"Dr. Kyra Fraser."

Kyra wanted to run across the stage and do cartwheels. But of course, she refrained from doing so. But, inside she was running, skipping, and jumping.

"Go, Kyra!"

"That's my baby girl!"

"Congrats, Ky."

As Kyra listened to them, she cried so hard she thought she would shake out her chair. She was ready to be with her family and friends. She was ready to get to the celebration party.

"That presents the graduating class of 2013," rambled the university president, as she brought the ceremony to a close.

As soon as the graduates were released to go, Kyra made her way in the direction she hoped her family would be. As she pushed her way through the crowd, she tried not to get tangled in her robe or lose her tam. Kyra saw an opening in the crowd and decided to move through it quickly when someone grabbed her elbow. Spinning around, she saw a familiar face.

"Oh, hey nephew. What are you doing?"

"I came to get you, Auntie. Everyone is over there," he said pointing.

"Okay, show me the way."

The two of them pushed their way through the crowd with Kyra's nephew leading the way. It was as though she had her own personal crowd parter. Making it safely to where her family was waiting, Kyra was excited to see them and immediately began to greet everyone with a hug.

"Hey, everybody! I'm glad you all made it. I'm so happy to see you all."

"We're so proud of you, Kyra."

"Thanks, Mom. Why are you crying? I thought I cried enough for everybody."

"I'm just glad to see that you are so happy. I knew you could do it, honey. I never doubted that for a minute. Kyra, look who's here."

"Jackie, you made it. It's been a long time since I've seen you girl."

"You know I wouldn't miss your big day for the world. You know you're my she-ro."

"Thanks for coming. Is everyone ready to party? Everybody knows how to get to the Marriot right?"

Everyone nodded and headed to their respective cars. Larkel took Kyra's hand and led her to his car.

"Lark, I'm so excited."

"Really? I couldn't tell."

"I see someone has jokes today. Aren't you excited?"

"Girl, you are excited enough for me, yourself, your mom, dad, brothers, nephews, cousins..."

"Cut it out. That's not funny."

"Baby, I'm just teasing you. Of course, I'm excited. I saw how hard you worked. You deserve this, honey."

Trying to get out of the parking lot was another ordeal. Then, Kyra began to feel anxious about the party.

"Let me call Vanessa and Eyana to see if they made it to the hotel."

"Honey, do you really think they wouldn't be there? Just relax. Everything will be fine. Enjoy the ride. We will be there soon."

Taking Lark at his word, Ky settled back into the soft leather of the seat and enjoyed the scenery and the joy of completing another milestone in her life.

Arriving to the hotel in a timely manner, Kyra walked into the expansive ballroom.

Oh, everything is absolutely beautiful. It's just how I imagined it would be. Everyone's here: my cousins, my friends, my neighbors, my classmates, and of course, my family.

"Hey, everybody. Thank you for coming. I'm so glad to see all of you," Eyana said greeting the guests.

"Kyra. Come sit over here. This is your table. Everyone, please find a seat. On the table, you will find a program. If you were asked to be on program, whether you are singing, speaking, dancing, or what have you, please look to see when you will be expected to come to the stage. Right now, the waiters are ready to serve the dinner salads. So, please enjoy your dinner, socialize, and I will be back before you soon."

"Eyana is doing a great job so far. Look at her. She doesn't seem nervous at all," Kyra whispered to her mother.

"After you put the pressure on her what did you think she was going to do?"

"Was I really too hard on her?"

"No, not really. You just expect excellence."

"And that's wrong?"

"No, but everyone has his/her own standard of excellence."

"And?"

"And, yours is just a little above most people's."

"Wow, they're playing one of my favorite cd's."

"Really, why don't you turn around and look."

"Oh, my God! Devo Called and Chosen! How were you guys able to get him?"

"Don't worry about all of that."

I'm so happy and filled with anxiousness for what the night will bring that I can barely eat. But the food smells incredibly. Um, this prime rib is really ender. This is delicious.

After taking a few bites, Kyra moved to the podium to say 'thank you' to her guests.

"Please continue to eat, while I say a few words of thank you. I would like to thank each and every one of you for coming out this evening and sharing this moment with me. As you all know, I have labored long and hard for this accomplishment, and I thank God that I can say there is light at the end of the tunnel. Conquering a task of this magnitude was by far no easy endeavor, and I could not have done it without a support group. All of you who are present here today were a part of that support group, whether you offered words of encouragement, lent an ear, or watched over my house and collected my mail while I was out of town. I love you, and I appreciate all that you have done that assisted in helping me to reach my goal. I want to give a special thanks to my parents for instilling in me the belief that "no weapon formed against me shall prosper" and that I can do "all things through Christ who strengthens me." They instilled in me a healthy self esteem which empowered me to be able to conquer mountains that appeared in my path. I would also like to thank my brothers and my sister-in-laws who never doubted that I could succeed at anything that I put my mind to. And to my girls, who always have my back. Thank you. And finally, to Larkel, my fiancé, thank you for your love and support and for going over all the research with me and for your constant encouragement. Now, please finish your meals and dessert will be served soon."

"Actually, we are going to continue with the program," Eyana interjected as she resumed her role as mistress of ceremonies. "Quantanique, Kyra's neice, would like to read a poem that she wrote for her auntie."

After Quantanique's beautiful poem, the program continued to move forward.

"Now, we are ready to present gifts to our guest of honor. Kyra, will you please come to the podium."

"All of you who have gifts to present may come forward at this time."

Why are they all huddling around in a big group like that? Why don't they form a line, so they will know who's going first? Why is everyone grinning from ear to ear? Something is going on. It seems like everyone is in on the inside joke, except me.

"Kyra?"

"Yes, Mom."

"The twelve of us, your dad and I, Larkel, August, Rod, Noah, Eyana, Tracy, James, Vanessa, Sandy, and Mrs. Sherten, would like to present this gift to you. With this gift, we are continuing to show our love for you and how proud we are to know you. We pray that you enjoy it and that it is everything that you wanted. Go ahead and open it."

"Thank you everybody. I'm so nervous that I can hardly get my fingers to cooperate. Oh, my God! A key. Is this for what I think it's for? Oh my God. It says Jaguar!"

"Well, honey. Let's go outside and see."

"Oh, my God! Oh, my God!"

"Let her through. Everybody follow us outside."

"My Jaguar! Oh, my God! Thank you! I love it! This is the best! Oh, my God!"

"I think she likes it everybody," Tracy said.

"You think?" James smirked.

Sitting outside, parked directly in the front entrance of the door sat a midnight blue Jaguar XJL with tan leather interior with a beautiful silver ribbon and bow neatly placed on the roof of the car. As Kyra walked around to the driver's side, she had tears running down her face. Onlookers began to stop to see what all the commotion was about. They began to cheer along with her family and friends. After taking a moment to admire her dream car, Kyra and her guests made their way back into the ballroom. All who wanted to share their expressions of love through words, gifts, hugs, and kisses did so once Kyra was back in her seat.

Chapter Twenty-Three

Returning to the office on Tuesday morning, Kyra didn't expect much had occurred or changed. As she walked in, Sandy greeted her as she was expecting her timely arrival.

"Good morning, boss."

"Oh, good morning, Sandy. You look well. How did everything go yesterday with your doctor appointment?"

"The doc says that everything is fine."

"Good. So, he gave you a clean bill of health?"

"Absolutely. So, did anything exciting happen while I was gone yesterday?"

"Actually, yes. I got a phone call from a quite eccentric individual. His name is Bishop Wallace Stratsford. And he has an appointment today."

"For what?"

"He says he wants to build a mega church."

"So, is he one of those religious fanatics?"

"No, I wouldn't say that, but he is passionate about God. That much I gathered from the conversation. But, I called him eccentric because of the way he speaks. He's just different."

"What time is he due to come in?"

"His appointment is for eleven o'clock. I'll buzz you when he comes in. Oh, by the way. That was a wonderful party Saturday night. Congratulations, doctor!"

"Thanks, Sandy. And thanks again for chipping in on the car. It's a dream come true."

I just need to finish this paper work, so that I can have a clear mind when Bishop Stratsford arrives for his appointment. I have a feeling that he is a punctual guy. I wonder if I should hire a new partner. I'm doing my work and the work Celeste used to do. Well, actually Sandy has been with me for so long that she knows how to do some of it, so she has been helping out. I could always give her additional responsibilities and a raise to go with it. That would save from having to hire an additional partner. Or, I could simply hire an accountant. Maybe, Lark and I could use the same accountant for both our businesses. Well, I guess sooner or later, I will have to make a decision about what is best for the firm.

"Sandy, I'm going to run to the ladies' room. If Bishop Stratsford comes in, seat him in my office."

Just as Kyra walked to the ladies' room, the main door opened and a well-dressed man walked in and approached Sandy's desk.

"Good morning, sir. How may I help you?"

"Good morning. I am the Bishop Stratsford, and I have an eleven o'clock engagement with a Ms. Fraser to discuss the construction for a mega church, which will be the new home of Missionary Lighthouse."

"Yes, it is a pleasure to meet you, Bishop. We spoke on the phone. Ms. Fraser will be with you momentarily. I can take you to her office if you like."

"I would very much appreciate that ma'am. And I didn't catch your name."

"My name is Sandy."

"Well, Sandy, it's always nice to meet a friendly and helpful assistant. Here is a brochure for our church. If you are ever in our area, feel free to be my guest."

"Thank you. I'll keep that in mind."

Before leaving the ladies' room, Kyra knew her guest had arrived because she could hear his deep and booming voice reverberating down the corridor. She braced herself for the unexpected as she walked into her office.

"Good morning. You must be Bishop Stratsford. I'm Kyra Fraser."

"Good morning, Ms. Fraser. It's nice to meet you. Are you ready to get down to business?"

"Absolutely. I need for you to try to create a mental image of what you are looking to create. But first, have you purchased the land?"

"Yes. Here are the documents that show the specifications."

"Great. Let me make a copy of this, so I can start your file."

"While you are doing that should I fill you in on how I want the floor plan of the building to be?"

"Absolutely. So, I see that you have given this some thought."

"This church has been in the works for over a year. At least mentally, it has."

"Tell me what you have in mind," Kyra said as she handed back the original document.

"These are the rooms that I want to have in the church. The main room of course will be the sanctuary. It should be able to house 1500-2000 people and have traditional pews that are stationary, not chairs. The floor for the sanctuary will have carpet, and we need a choir stand with seats, enough for 100 people."

"Will you want special lighting for the choir stand? And will you have a stationary podium or a moveable one?"

"Yes, we will need special lighting for the choir stand, preferably ones that don't put out a lot of heat. And as far as the podium is concerned, we will have a portable one."

"What's the next room?'

"The kitchen. It should be large enough to house three large industrial refrigerators, have two stoves, and double ovens."

"What about flooring?"

"Maybe you can give me some ideas on that later."

"No problem. What's next?"

"Bathrooms. We want two near the front foyer and two near the rear."

"Do you want private bathrooms or ones with stalls?"

"Once we determine the dimensions for the primary rooms, we can decide that based upon the space that's available."

"Sounds good. What's next?"

"We need a nursery that should be able to hold three cribs and enough floor space for other toddlers to play. It will also need to have room for a toy box and two changing tables."

"Great. What about offices?"

"Yes, we will need three offices of varying sizes and a sound room to house the electrical equipment."

"Do you have the specs for the offices or should we fill in the details later?"

"We can fill in the details later. There are just two more rooms that I want: the fellowship hall, which should be towards the rear of the church and a youth center, which should have classrooms and be on the same property but not attached to the main building."

"Are there any other rooms that you want?"

"No. Those will be sufficient. I will go now and let you do what you're so good at. When can I expect your call?"

"I will have my secretary call you in a week or two to set an appointment when the drafts are done."

"Great. I will be expecting your call."

Wow! Talk about prepared. This job is going to be a cinch. He knows exactly what he wants and where he wants it. He is an architect's dream client. I'm going to have this project sewed up in no time. Now, let me input the specs into the computer and close down for the day.

"Sandy, I'm going to leave for the day. Were you able to make the reservation on the Princess for Tracy's baby shower?"

"Yes, but only because someone had to cancel a reservation. At this late date getting a reservation on that boat was hard to come by."

"Well, I'm glad you were able to pull it off. Tracy is going to love this. I'll see you bright and early in the morning."

Chapter Twenty-Four

The day finally arrived for Tracy's baby shower. Instead of personally taking her gift with her to the shower, Kyra had the store deliver the item to the dock where the ship was stationed.

All the ladies, who were either helping with the setup or either coming as guests, were excited about participating in the shower and getting an opportunity to see Jasmeen for the first time.

When Kyra arrived, she immediately began working. As she moved about the room, she noticed a puddle under the ice sculpture.

"Stephanie, your sister is going to kill you if you let that ice sculpture melt. That was the one thing that she requested for the baby shower."

"I know. This is not a day to piss Tracy off. I'm trying to figure out how I can keep this thing from melting all over the floor. Oh, I'll plug up those fans and move them over here. This should work."

"Yeah, girl. Work it out."

"Oh hush, Ky. You could lend me a hand."

"Does it look like I have a free hand? I have to hurry up and get these decorations up before everyone starts to show up. If you knew how much they charge per hour for this boat, you would hurry up too."

"I think I get the point. I'm hurrying."

As the ladies worked, the guests began to arrive. First, Vanessa and Mrs. Fraser arrived, bringing refreshments and the cake. Not long after, the two guests of honors arrived just as the final touches were put in place. Kyra immediately ran over and took Jasmeen from Tracy.

"Oh, let me see my baby," she swooned.

"Well, hello to you too, Kyra," Tracy said half-jokingly.

"I'm sorry, Tracy. How are you?"

"I am doing great, just a little tired."

"It looks like motherhood really agrees with you."

"Thanks, sweetie. That means a lot to me."

"You're welcome. Everyone's coming in. Come over here and have a seat with Jasmeen."

More and more women poured into the space with gifts in hand. Tracy was excited to see what Jazz would receive. Due to Jazz's early arrival, Tracy didn't have time to complete her shopping list for all the items needed for the nursery.

As Tracy greeted her guests, Ky admired her glow of motherhood. After everyone settled in, Kyra and Vanessa proceeded with the games. The ladies laughed, ate and had a great time. Finally, it was time to see what was inside all of the beautifully wrapped packages.

"Okay, ladies. It's time for Tracy to open Jasmeen's gifts. Ready, Trace?"

"You know it girl. Bring them on. Okay. This first one is from Vanessa. This is just what I need, a stroller, and it's pink and baby green. This is beautiful. Thanks, Nessa."

"No problem, girl."

"The next gift is from my big sister Steph. A Winnie-the-Pooh high chair. That was definitely on my list. Thanks, Steph. Jazz, tell Auntie thank you. Next, we have a gift from my sister-in-law Tiana. Look Jazz, you can get your walk on with this girl. Oh, and this walker has toys built into it. It's an all in one center. Thanks, T."

"You're welcome, Tracy. Anything for my first niece."

"What's next?"

"Open this one. This is from me, Tracy."

"Thanks, Sandy. Oh, wow! These are beautiful. These sleepers will keep her warm. Look at these little dresses. Oh, they are complete outfits with shoes and socks and even the hair accessories."

"Well, we have to train her right. Don't we?"

"Amen to that."

"This next gift is from my mom, Tracy."

"Thanks, Mrs. Fraser. These are beautiful blankets. Did you make these?"

"I made the crocheted one, but the one with the little pillow and bumper pad came from the store."

"Open the big box."

"I'm going to need help with this one. Kyra, come over here."

"My pleasure. This is from Larkel and me."

"Oh, thank you. It's the crib that I showed you. How were you able to get it?"

"They deliver from the east coast."

"You went to all that trouble?"

"It was no trouble at all. You know I would do anything for my best friend."

"I love you, Ky."

"I love you, too, Trace."

"Awe they're getting all mushy."

"Here sweetie. These two gifts are from me and James' mom," said Tracy's mother.

"Thanks mom one and mom two. How thoughtful. She's really going to need these accounts."

"One is for her college fund and the other is for what she wants to use it for when she gets older." After the last gift was opened, Kyra noticed the time and sprang to her feet.

"I don't mean to rush everyone, but we need to start cleaning up and start putting all the gifts in the back of the SUV. We have about forty-five minutes to clear out of here."

"Thank you everyone for coming. James told me to tell you all 'thank you' from the bottom of his heart for all that you have done for us and our baby. We love you all."

"You're welcome, girl. Group hug."

Chapter Twenty-Five

(A week later)

Lark's grand opening was successful, my graduation was a blast, and Tracy's baby shower was overall a lot of fun. Jasmeen has already been born, so the only thing left in our immediate plans is the wedding. I can't believe this is actually going to take place. We have been so busy that we haven't really been able to talk about it, but at least the plans are moving ahead. Mom has been doing her part. Her only daughter is getting married, so you can believe that this will be the wedding of the year, if she has anything to say about it. As a matter of fact, I'm waiting for her now. She's coming to pick me up to take me to get fitted for my dress. Marcella said she is almost finished, but she needs me to try it on before she puts on the finishing touches. I'm having my dress custom made. I have imagined how my dress would look for years now, even before I met Larkel.

Speaking of Larkel, I hope he will alter his schedule for next semester. If he continues like he's going now, he will always be tired. He won't have much energy outside of work and barely enough for that.

Hearing her mother's car pulling up, Kyra grabbed her sweater and met her outside.

"Good morning, Mom. You're looking radiant. What gives?"

"It could be my new face cream, or it could be the fact that my baby is getting married. Honey, I'm so proud of you. You are the dream daughter that every mother wants."

"Really? I didn't hear you singing my praises when I was a teenager and giving you premature gray hair."

"You were just being the typical teenager."

"That's what you say now, Mom. Do you remember how to get to Marci's?"

"She's right off the 15 freeway, right? I was over there just the other day to take her the money to get the supplies for your dress. Remember?"

"That's right. I'm sorry. I've been a little preoccupied lately."

"That's okay, dear. Is something wrong?"

"No, not really. I'm just concerned about Larkel. He's been working really hard, and he's always exhausted."

"Well, his tech center has only been open for a couple of months. He's running off adrenaline."

"I know, and when that burns out that's exactly what he's going to have- burn out."

"He'll be okay, honey."

"I hope so, Mom. I really hope so."

"We're here, honey. Let's go in. I believe she has another appointment after us."

Marcella is an excellent seamstress. I love the details of my gown. It looks even more beautiful than I could have ever dreamed. Not to be conceited, but I am going to be a very beautiful bride. Wow! She even made accessories for my hair and for all the bridesmaids and the matron of honor. What until they see these. They are going to be ecstatic. Everything is gorgeous.

"How does it feel?" Marci asked Kyra as she surveyed her seam work.

"It feels wonderful. I don't want to take it off. You have done a marvelous job. This is far better than I expected. I don't mean your abilities; I mean this is much more than I imagined."

"Well, you only get married once, right?"

"That's the plan."

"And, I'm not finished. I still need to put all the decorations on the bodice. I'll give you a moment to let your mom help you out of it."

"Thanks, Marci."

After taking off the wedding gown and nearly running from Marcella's, Kyra jumped in her mom's car anxious to get back to her own car. She needed to get to the office. There was much work to do. Once she made it home, she didn't bother to go inside; she kissed her mother goodbye, jumped into her car and made her way to the freeway.

Off to the office I go. I need to begin drafting the plans for the mega church. I only have about three hours to put into it. Larkel is picking me up at five o'clock sharp. I didn't get a chance to hang out with him this past weekend because of the baby shower, so I am really looking forward to seeing my honey.

"Good afternoon, Sandy," Kyra said as she tried to walk quickly past Sandy's desk. She didn't have a minute to spare for small talk.

"Good afternoon, boss. How was the fitting?"

"Sandy, everything was absolutely gorgeous. I can't even begin to describe how beautiful the dress is. Marcella is fantastic. You wouldn't imagine anyone could create such beauty," Kyra answered, not able to resist an opportunity to discuss her beautiful gown.

"What do you think you do here?"

"Yeah, well I guess everyone has his/her own talent. And you should see the hair accessories that she made for the bridal party. The girls are going to go crazy when they see what she has made for them."

"Sounds exciting. I can't wait for the big day. Three weeks will go by before we know it."

"I know. Well, I'll be in my drafting room if anyone needs me. Is James in his office?"

"You just missed him. He's on his way to the Wheaton/Pearce property."

"As soon as I get a free moment I'm going to drive over there and see how everything is coming together."

After placing her personal items in her office, Kyra immediately made her way to her drafting room to begin hammering away on the Stratsford project.

What is wrong with this computer? I know I saved the specs for the Stratsford project. Where is it? Tell me this isn't happening. The last thing I need is to have to call Bishop Stratsford and tell him that I don't have the information that he took almost two hours to give me. This job could fall right from under me. Maybe I named it something else. What though? What did he say the name of the church is? Where are my notes? God, help me. Give me a sign. Missionary Lighthouse. That's it. Here it is. Now, what possessed me to save it under that rather than his name, which is procedure? Time to get down to business.

Drafting has always been a way for me to relax and to let my imagination flow freely. It's almost like entering another world. Let me take a step back and look at what I've accomplished on the Stratsford Project. Hmm, looks like a one-story dollhouse. I'm sure the congregation is going to love their new church home. What time is it? Oh my, it's a quarter to five. I need to clean up, so I can be ready when Lark gets here. The last thing I want to do is have the man sitting around after he's been working hard all day. You know how it is after you've been working hard and then you sit still. Your body thinks it's time to wind down, and eventually, you get sleepy.

"Sandy, let me know right away when Lark arrives. I'm clearing up the drafts right now."

"No problem, boss. What time are you expecting him?"

"He should be here at five sharp. You know, on second thought, I'll just go downstairs and meet him in front."

"Do you want me to finish placing the drafts in the portfolio?"

"That would be a big help, Sandy. I'll just grab my purse. I'll see you in the morning."

"Have fun, kiddo."

"We will."

Kyra arrived downstairs at exactly five minutes before the hour. However, at five o'clock, Larkel had not made his arrival. By five minutes after, Kyra had begun to grow anxious.

It's fifteen after five. I wonder where he could be. This is not like Lark to be late and not call. Let me call upstairs and see if he has spoken to Sandy. Maybe he's stuck in traffic.

"Sandy, has Lark called?"

"No, he hasn't. Where are you?"

"I'm still downstairs."

"Well, have you tried his cell phone?"

"Yes, but there's no answer. I also tried his house and the tech center. He's not at either."

"Well, what are you going to do now? Are you sure you weren't supposed to meet him at the restaurant?"

"Yes, I'm sure. He was going to take me to a new spot. It was going to be a surprise. Maybe I'll just go home and wait for him to call. It's getting cold out here."

"Okay, Kyra. Let me know if there is anything I can do to help."

"Well, you will be leaving in fifteen minutes yourself. Go home to your husband. I'm sure everything will work out. I'll see you in the morning."

It's eight-thirty, and I still haven't heard from Lark. I am really worried. I don't want to call his mom because I don't want to scare her. I'm sure if anything were wrong, she would have called to let me know. I just can't imagine what is going on. I'll just lie here until I hear something. I know I should eat, but I feel kind of nauseous, like something is seriously wrong.

Kyra runs the possible reasons for Lark's tardiness through her mind. The ring of her cell phone interrupts her thoughts.

"Lark!"

"No, Ky. It's me Tracy. What's wrong?"

"Oh, I guess I was asleep. I was waiting for Lark to call."

"You must have had an awesome time last night."

"Last night? What time is it?"

"It's seven-thirty in the morning. Is everything alright?"

"No, Trace. It's Lark. We never went to dinner. He never picked me up from work, and I haven't heard from him. I don't know what's going on..."

"Slow down, Ky. Have you called his mom?"

"No. Look, I'm going to try his cell again, and I'll call you back."

Kyra immediately disconnected from the call and dialed Larkel's phone.

"Hello?" a strange voice answered.

"Hello? Who is this? Did I dial 909-555-1000?"

"I'm not sure, but this is Doctor Langston. Are you calling for Larkel Sherten?"

"Yes, what's going on?"

"I'm sorry ma'am, but there has been an accident. May I ask to whom I am speaking and what your relationship is to Dr. Sherten?"

"My name is Kyra Fraser, and I am his fiancée. What's going on? You said there was an accident."

"Maybe you should come down to Mercy General."

"Can you give me any information? Is he okay?"

"He was involved in a car accident. He's unconscious right now. It may be best if you come down to the hospital."

"I'm on my way."

Kyra frantically searches for her keys as she dials Lark's mother's phone number.

"Mrs. Sherten?"

"Yes, Kyra. Good morning."

"Can you meet me in the front of your house in ten minutes? Larkel was in a car accident, and we need to go to the hospital."

"Oh, my God. Is he okay?"

"All I know is that he is unconscious. I just found out myself. Can you be ready in ten minutes?"

"I'll be ready in three."

"I'm on my way."

Chapter Twenty-Six

When Kyra and Mrs. Sherten arrived to the hospital, they immediately went to the emergency room.

"We're here to see Larkel Sherten. I'm his fiancée, and this is his mother."

"Come with me."

"Oh, my God, Mom! Look at him!" Kyra exclaimed as the tears rolled down her face.

"It's okay, Kyra. I don't think it's as bad as it looks. Nurse, where is the doctor?"

"He's on his way."

"He's still not awake. What happened? I want some answers."

"I can help you with that. I'm Dr. Langston. It seems that Dr. Sherten fell asleep at the wheel, and there was a head-on collision. According to the person who was in the other car, he came over to his side of the street. He has suffered some internal bleeding, and he has a broken leg. Thank God he was wearing his seatbelt, or it could have been much worse. His vital signs are good. We're just waiting for him to awaken. I'm glad you called his cell phone when you did. We had been hoping ever since he was brought in yesterday that someone would call because we did not have an emergency contact."

"How's the other driver doing?"

"He will be okay. He's awake and actually he was released last night."

"Thank God. Is it okay if we sit here until he wakes up?"

"Sure. I'll bring in an extra chair."

"Kyra, clean your face. All is well. I'm sure he will wake up soon, and I'm sure you don't want to greet him with bloodshot eyes."

I'd better call Sandy and Trace and let them know where I am. I better call my mother too while I'm at it, just in case she calls looking for me. Thank you, Lord for not letting me get worse news on the end of the phone. Everything has been going great. I told Larkel. Why didn't he listen to me? This is definitely a warning for him. I wonder if the doctor checked his brain waves. I wonder if he will be okay mentally and physically.

A couple of hours later, Lark began to moan as if he was trying to talk, but he still had his eyes closed. Kyra began to gently message his arm and signaled to his mother to get the closest attendant.

"Ky, is that you?" Lark asked as he strained to open his eyes. "Where are we?"

"Sweetie, don't try to move. Your mom and I are here. You're in the hospital. You were in a car accident. Honey, do you remember anything?"

"The last thing I remember was being on my way to pick you up to go to dinner. Ow, my head."

"Honey, lay back. Don't try to move. The doctor will be right here. I'm so happy that you're okay. You really scared me," Kyra said as the tears began to roll down her face again.

"I'll be alright, baby. Don't cry. Did I hurt anyone?"

"The doctor said that there was another car involved, but the guy was discharged last night. He only suffered minor scrapes and bruises."

"Dr. Sherten, it's good to see you awake. You've been asleep for eighteen hours. How do you feel?"

"Groggy and sore."

"That's to be expected. I'm going to do a secondary routine check over your entire body to make sure that there isn't anything that went undetected. Is that okay with you, Dr. Sherten?"

"Absolutely, do whatever you need to do."

"Can you tell me who our current president is?

"Barack Hussein Obama."

"Excellent."

"Is there anything I should know about my condition?"

"You suffered internal bleeding, and you have a broken leg. I will order additional tests to be done and get back to you just as soon as the results are in," the doctor said before walking out.

"How am I supposed to walk down the aisle with a broken leg? We're getting married in three weeks."

"Honey, let's not worry about the wedding right now. We need to get you all fixed up. Babe, your mom is here. I think she's talking to the doctor. Let me call her in."

"Mom Sherten, Lark wants to see you. Did the doctor say whether or not he would be released today?"

"Once they get the results of the tests they will run, they will be able to let us know. Let me go see my baby."

Thank you, Lord for allowing him to be alive. I know the damage could have been so much worse. Some people have head-on collisions and don't live to tell about it, and others end up being vegetables. I thank you for watching over him. I don't know what I'd do if he weren't here with me.

"Ms. Fraser?"

"Yes, doctor?"

"Dr. Sherten will be released later this evening. Of course, he's going to need a ride.

Before then, the police will come in to take a report."

"Thank you, doctor. Is there a prescription that I can get filled while I'm waiting?"

"As a matter of fact, I was going to my office to write it out. I'm going to give him something for the pain. Oh, and you will notice some bruising on him. It may last for a couple of weeks or so."

"Larkel, the doctor says that you can be released this evening. I'm going to go and get your prescription filled and pick up some of your things from your place and take them over to mine, so that you will be comfortable. I guess this was one way to get you to slow down."

"Don't be so hard on me, Ky. I know I messed up, but…"

"Don't you know that I need you here with me?" Kyra said as tears once again filled her eyes.

"Honey, I know. I'm sorry. I should have taken your advice. In a couple of days, I will have things rearranged at the tech center."

"Lark, I just want the best for you. You know that, right?"

"Of course, honey. That's why I love you."

"I'll be back in a couple of hours. Mom, are you staying or do you want a ride back?"

"I'll go with you, so I can get my car. Then, I'll come right back. I'll sit with him while you're gone. Then, when you come to get him you won't have to worry about dropping me off."

"Okay, baby. We'll see you later. Don't go too far."

"I don't think I have much of a choice."

Chapter Twenty-Seven

(Two months later)

Larkel finally had his cast removed last week; he had to wear it for six weeks. He has lightened his workload by delegating more responsibility to his staff and the new accountant. He and Kyra decided to get an accountant, one they can share for both their businesses.

The wedding is back on. They will say their vows to each other in two weeks.

I can't wait. While Lark was staying with me, it gave me a taste of what married life is like. It's going to take some getting used to, but so far I believe he is definitely worth devoting my life to.

Both our mothers are excited again and are looking forward to the big day. Dad is a little nervous about walking me down the aisle, but he'll never admit it. The bridal party and the groomsmen went for their fittings last weekend. Everyone is in a festive mood.

As far as the firm is concerned, everything is moving right along. Sandy and James have been helping out more because I had to split my time between home and the office to make sure Larkel was taking his medicine to keep the pain down and that everything he needed was within his reach. And I had to go to the tech center to check on things there. His mother was a big help. She came over at least three times a week to help out. My mom even came to help out some too.

The Wheaton and Pearce projects are complete. They have invited me to their grand, grand opening, but I think it's set for the same weekend as the wedding, so I guess that means I won't be there.

The Stratsford project is still in the construction stage and will be for another few months at least. The bishop is pleased with how everything is going, so I don't have to worry about undue changes.

Enough daydreaming, I need to get dressed for the engagement dinner. This is an exclusive dinner for immediate family members and the wedding party only. It's sort of a pre-celebration dinner. I have gifts for all of the bridal party and my parents, and Lark has gifts for his guys and his mom.

Once they arrive to the restaurant, Mrs. Fraser gives Kyra a once over.

"Hi, sweetie. How are you feeling?"

"I'm fine, Mom."

"You look a little tired, honey. How much rest have you been getting?"

"Well, the last couple of months have been rough, but things are getting back to normal now that Larkel is back on full duty at the center."

"Have you thought about taking some time off before the wedding?"

"Before the wedding? Why would I do that? We're going to be gone for a week after the wedding. I can't be gone from the firm too long, Mom."

"I understand dear, but if you go on your honeymoon tired, you won't be able to enjoy yourself. You'll be too tired."

"I'll keep that in mind. Where are we sitting?"

"We have a private room reserved in the back. Where's Lark?"

"He saw some of the guys when we came in, so maybe they went in already."

Finally making her way to the private room, Kyra began to speak to the guests.

"Hey, everybody. I'm sorry to keep everyone waiting."

"We know you just wanted to make a grand entrance, girl. Save it for the wedding."

"Yeah, girl. Have you been practicing your strut? You know you better practice walking in your shoes. It's nothing like breaking in a new pair of heels."

"I hadn't thought of that. I guess I figured I would put them on the day of the wedding and as you said strut down the aisle. I guess I better break them in a little."

"That's what bridesmaids are for- to keep you on your toes."

"What would I do without my girls?"

"If you keep being nice to us you may never have to find out."

"Cute, Trace. Real cute."

"She's just being real with you, Ky."

"What else would you expect from her, Nessa?"

"Nothing but the truth and only the truth."

Anxious to get the evening started, Lark turned to Kyra and asked, "Honey, do you want to start off or should I?"

"Lark, you go ahead and do the honors."

"First, we would like to thank all of you for joining us in celebrating our impending wedding and marriage. This is a day that I have looked forward to for many years even prior to meeting Kyra. I just needed that special someone to share it with, and here she is. Also, I want to thank those of you who are in the wedding party for taking out your time to support us with your presence and the commitment that you have made to making this day special not only for me and Ky but for all of us. Ky, would you like to speak to the group now?"

"Absolutely. I just want to add to what Larkel has said. I thank each and every one of you for loving and caring for us enough to take this journey with us. I don't see it as you helping out for only one day, but serving as a network that will be there in the time of need and joy. I want to especially thank Lark's mom for raising such a respectable man who is worthy of love and admiration. If it weren't for what his parents planted in him, he wouldn't be the man he is today. So, I thank you Mrs. Sherten for doing such a wonderful job. And to my parents, I love you, and I thank you for being examples for me to look up to and respect. You both have always been pillars of strength and have always stood by me in the choices that I have made. Thank you."

"Is everyone ready to order? The waiter has been waiting patiently, so Kyra how about letting everyone eat while the night is still young."

"Sounds good. And if anyone has anything you want to share while we eat feel free."

Chapter Twenty-Eight

It's my wedding day, and I haven't stopped crying all night and all morning. My mom is trying to help me position the tiara in front of this updo that Lamar hooked up for me, and Tracy is fussing over my makeup. Lillie, Lark's sister, is trying to find the Visine, so it can help get the red out of my eyes, so I don't scare the guests. I don't want them to think I'm sad, nor do I want to mess up the wedding photos. I can't wait to see Lark. I know he is going to be the best looking groom ever. I wonder where Vanessa is. I haven't seen or heard from her all morning, but Trace says not to worry.

Speak of the devil. I hear her coming up the stairs now.

"Nessa, where have you been?"

"Well, it took me a little while to find the something blue. But leave it to me, I found it."

"So, what did you get? Are you just going to keep Kyra waiting? She's already in a frenzy."

"Slow down, Trace. Did you guys already do the ritual?"

"Sort of. Her mom gave her the something new, the tiara. I have the something old, this antique wedding album. I hope you like it, Ky."

"It's absolutely beautiful, Tracy."

"Oh, my God. There go the waterworks again. We really need to cut this out."

"And, Kyra I have the something borrowed. It's a satin handkerchief that my mom gave me when I went off to college."

"That's exactly what she needs. And girl, I have the something blue. It's the garter belt. There is a blue one and a white one."

"Oh, that's perfect, Vanessa. I had totally forgotten about the tradition of throwing the garter belt."

"Yeah, but here is the one you will throw, and the blue one is for you to keep."

"Thank all of you. Am I presentable yet?"

"A couple more drops of Visine and you'll be ready."

"Mom, what do you think?"

"You look absolutely beautiful, honey. Now, I am going to go downstairs and take my seat and let your dad know to meet you in the hallway by the garden entrance."

"Okay, girls let's do this."

"Yeah, let's get you married."

Everything was so beautiful and exquisite. Kyra never imagined everything would be so green and colorful, but that is why she figured springtime would be the best time to have a wedding outdoors. Well, it's summer now and everything is still green and gorgeous.

As Kyra stood in her concealed spot, she watched the wedding begin. From what she could see, all the guests looked lovely with their beautiful smiles. She wished she could see her mom, but her spot did not lend a good view. She watched all her girls, in their individually designed dresses, walk in. Tracy was the first to walk down the aisle as the matron of honor. She was of course coupled with the best man, Martin, who is Lark's best friend. Then, Vanessa walked in, who was coupled with Richard. And finally, the second bridesmaid and groomsman, Lillie and Spencer. Next, the two flower girls sauntered in: Kimara and Tsehai. They were so beautiful and precious, Kyra almost started crying. She noticed they seemed a little shy, but they were doing a wonderful job.

Okay, it's my turn.

"Okay, honey. Are you ready? Everyone's standing. As you always say, 'Let's get this show on the road.'"

"Yes, Daddy. I'm ready."

"You know, no matter how old you get, you will always be my little girl."

"I know, Daddy. I know."

When Kyra took her place on her father's arm, she looked past all the guests and focused her attention on the altar.

Lark looks amazing. I just want to run into his arms right now. But I must exercise some self-constraint.

After stating the preliminary words spoken at the beginning of a traditional wedding ceremony, the pastor gave the couple an opportunity to speak from their hearts, "Now the lovely couple will share the personal vows that they have written for each other."

"Kyra, I have waited for you for years. And when you suddenly appeared before me in the spa and again in your office, it was a dream come true. I couldn't explain it at the time, but I felt an instant connection to you and that connection has grown and become clearer throughout the time that we have been together. I love you dearly, and I know that it is just the beginning of how deep I will love you in the years to come. I cherish you, for you are my queen. I pledge my life and my love to you on this day, and I promise to love you throughout the days of our lives. I promise to not only be your husband but your best friend, one who will be there through the good times and the bad. And I promise that your days of happiness will be infinite."

"Larkel, I have met my match. We compliment each other in so many ways that it's unbelievable: in spirit, in character, in humor, and in love. I have met my match. For me, you are the perfect mate. Nothing fits better than a hand and glove, except for a man and his wife. And today, as I pledge my undying love to you by becoming your wife and taking you as my husband, I'm telling you that I will work together with you to help to make a perfect fit. The day that I first saw you, something pulled at my heart, and I knew that if the right opportunity came along that I would be all yours. And that day came, and it led us to today. Larkel, I pledge my love to you for today and always. I promise to always stand by you and to fill your life with happiness and unspeakable joy, as we journey down this road of marriage."

"And with these pledges, I now pronounce you husband and wife. Larkel, you may now kiss your bride. To all of the guests, it is my pleasure to present to you, Dr. and Dr. Larkel Sherten."

Oh, my God. I actually made it through the ceremony without fainting from joy.

"Lark, are you excited?" Kyra whispered as they turned and faced their guests.

"No, Ky. I'm just normal," Lark whispered back.

"That's not funny, Lark."

"Oh, yes it is. Why would you ask me a silly question like that? This silly grin that I'm wearing should tell you that I'm excited."

"I just wanted to hear you tell me. And your grin is not silly. I love your smile."

"Thanks, honey. And you look absolutely beautiful in that dress. Man, I am so lucky."

By that time, the newlyweds had made it outside the front doors of the church.

"Okay you love birds. Can anyone else talk to you? You guys have plenty of time to talk later."

"Mom, I was just admiring my bride. Isn't she drop-dead gorgeous?"

"Of course, Larkel. He's right, Kyra. You are more beautiful than ever. Let's go inside and greet all of your guests."

I need to sit down. Even though I walked around in these shoes as Tracy suggested, they are still doing a number on my feet. I'll just sit here and look pretty and let everyone come over to the head table. That's allowed right?

After all the guests filed into the reception and took their assigned seats, the toasting began. After the best man and matron of honor gave their toasts, Kyra's father was next in line.

"I'd like to give a toast to the bride and the groom. I must say, Kyra once again you never cease to amaze me. If someone could find a man that was truly her equal, it would be my baby girl. Honey, once again I am so proud of you, and I wish you and Larkel the best in all that you do. I love both of you. Larkel, welcome to the family, son. It's good to have another son on board."

By the end of the evening, Ky and Lark were ready to get on with the honeymoon.

All the photos have been taken, all the food has been devoured, and the dances have been danced. I didn't know that people paid this much money to dance with the bride. I have twenties, fifties, and even a couple of hundred dollar bills pinned to my wedding dress. This is great.

Now that we have kissed everyone bon voyage, my husband and I are off to our honeymoon. We are on our way to the Caribbean, thanks to my parents. And we will shop till we drop, thanks to Lark's mom.

Well, as I always say, "Let's get this show on the road!"

Chapter Twenty-Nine
(A week later)

After the honeymooners returned home, they began to move from their respective residences into their brand new home. When Kyra went into her bedroom, she instructed the movers to be very careful with the dresser. As they pulled it away from the wall, from the corner of her eye, she saw something white lying against the edge of the wall. She leaned over to pick it up. It was a business card.

Dr. Larkel Sherten
Professor of Computer Technology
University of California, Riverside
909.555.1000

the card read. All Kyra could do was laugh.

Gift of Salvation
for
Non-Believers

"For all have sinned, and come short of the glory of God."
Romans 3:23

This section was written especially for non-believers, those who have not accepted the gift of salvation. The gift of salvation saves souls from eternal damnation and is a free gift offered by God himself. John 3:16-18 says, *"For God so loved the world, that he gave his only begotten Son, that whosoever believeth in him should not perish, but have everlasting life. For God sent not his Son into the world to condemn the world; but that the world through him might be saved. He that believeth on him is not condemned: but he that believeth not is condemned already, because he hath not believed in the name of the only begotten Son of God."* This section of scripture tells us God's purpose for giving His son Jesus to the world. The world was in a bad condition. The world was overwrought with sin; the people were living for fleshly desires rather than for God's desires.

As a result of the world's conditions, God decided that He would offer the perfect sacrifice that would save the world from being a place where people were lost and had no hope. He decided that His own son could stand in proxy for the sin-filled world, taking all sin upon Himself.

So Jesus came, born of a virgin, to save this dying world. He walked on this earth for 33 ½ years, doing the work of His Heavenly Father. At the appointed time, He died by way of crucifixion upon a cross at Calvary, on Golgatha's hill. He shed his blood and died for you and for me. Because His blood was pure, it paid the penalty for all unrighteousness and gave those who believe in Him direct access to His father's throne.

Scripture tells us in Matthew 27:51 that the veil of the temple was ripped in two from top to bottom, at the moment that Jesus' spirit left His body. As a result of the veil's removal, we are no longer required to have a high priest make intercession for us. We, as the children of the Most High God, are able to approach the throne God for ourselves, and Jesus sits on the right hand of the Father making intercession for us.

But what is even more miraculous than God offering His own son as the perfect sacrifice was the fact that when Jesus was placed in grave clothes and placed in a tomb, He only remained there until the third day. God would not have it that His son would remain in the heart of the earth forever. In order for people to believe in the awesome power of God and His dear son Jesus, a miracle had to be performed. So, on the third day, after Jesus died on the cross, He was resurrected, demonstrating the omnipotence of God. This very act was the act that would cause people to believe in a god that reigns supreme and holds the power of the universe in His very hands, a god that could save them from themselves.

Today, if you are an unbeliever, you can change your destiny. You can change where you will spend your eternity. Our Heavenly Father gives us the freedom of choice about how we want to live our life here on earth and how we want to spend eternity. In Deuteronomy 30:19, God boldly declares, *"I call heaven and earth to record this day against you, that I have set before you life and death, blessing and cursing: therefore choose life, that both thou and thy seed may live."*

So, dear friend what choice will you make today? Will you spend your eternity with the Creator or will you suffer Hell's eternal flames? Again, the choice is yours. Just as the men aboard the ship who were with Jonah became believers, you too can make a choice to accept the only one and true living God as your god.

If after reading the above passages, you have decided that you want to spend your eternity in Heaven with God, the creator, and His son Jesus, and the Holy Spirit, read through what has affectionately come to be known as the Roman's Road. This is the road to salvation. As you read through the scriptures that comprise the Roman's Road, you will also read the explanation for each scripture so you will have clarity about what you are reading and confessing.

The Roman's Road to Salvation

The road to salvation begins with Romans 3:23 which declares, *"For all have sinned, and come short of the glory of God."* This scripture explains that everyone has come short of God's glory and needs redemption. Then Romans 6:23a states, "*For the wages of sin is death.*" Here, we learn that the consequence of living a life of sin is death. Everyone will experience physical death as a result of the sin committed in the garden of Eden, but those who commit themselves to a life of sin will suffer eternal damnation in the lake of fire (Rev. 19).

Continue with the rest of verse 6:23 that says, "*but the gift of God is eternal life through Jesus Christ our Lord.*" There is an alternative to suffering eternal damnation. We can accept the gift of salvation by accepting Jesus as our personal lord and savior. Then, Romans 5:8 says, "*But God commendeth his love toward us, in that, while we were yet sinners, Christ died for us.*" We are able to receive the gift of salvation because Christ came to earth and shed His blood for us on the cross.

Continue to Romans 10: 9-10 which says, "*That if thou shalt confess with thy mouth the Lord Jesus, and shalt believe in thine heart that God hath raised him from the dead, thou shalt be saved. For with the heart man believeth unto righteousness; and with the mouth confession is made unto salvation.*" If we confess with our mouths that Jesus is the son of God, that he came and died for our sins, and that God raised Him from the dead, we will receive salvation.

Finish with Romans 10:13, which states, "*For whosoever shall call upon the name of the Lord shall be saved.*" Call upon the name of God by saying these words, "**Lord Jesus, come into my heart and save me Lord. I believe that you are the Son of God who came and died on the cross for my sins. I believe that you rose from the grave. I also** believe that you now sit in heaven on the right side of the Father, making intersession for me. I accept you as my Lord and my Savior."

Now that you have confessed with your mouth that Jesus is the son of God and that He died for our sins and rose from the grave, **YOU ARE NOW SAVED!!!!** You will spend your eternity in heaven.

The next step is very important- you must find a bible-based church that teaches the word of God and confesses the Lord Jesus Christ to be the son of God. Don't delay. Do this immediately. Do not leave yourself open to the enemy. Get connected with the saints of the Most High God and keep yourself covered with the unspotted blood of the lamb.

Here is my prayer for you.

Father God,

I thank you for the opportunity to minister your word to the unsaved, the unchurched, and the uncommitted. Father God, I pray now for the souls who have just received the gift of salvation. Lord Father, they have opened their hearts to you, and I know that you have received them into your kingdom and written their names in the Book of Life. Father God, I pray that you will touch their lives and show yourself mightily before them. Let their eyes be opened by the scales falling off, allowing them to see clearly.

Father God, I even pray for the backslider, those who have turned away from you after receiving the gift of salvation. You said in your word that you desire that none would perish. So Lord, I send your word to them right now praying that they would confess the iniquity in their heart, repent, and turn from their evil ways, so that they may receive a life of abundance. You said in your word in Matthew Chapter 14, that every knee shall bow before you and every tongue will confess that Jesus is Lord.

Father God, I pray now that we all come under subjection to your word and that we will humbly submit our lives to you. I ask all these things in the name of my Lord and Savior Jesus Christ.
Amen, Amen, Amen!!!!

I will continue to pray for your success in your walk with God. Remember, this spiritual walk that you are about to embark on will not be an easy walk, but remember, the race is not given to the swift but to those who endure to the end.

Be blessed with heaven's best. I love you!

ABOUT THE AUTHOR

Dr. Cassundra White-Elliott resides in California with her family, where as an English/Education professor she works for various community colleges and universities. One of the universities she teaches for is the Southern California Branch of the University of Phoenix. There she teaches communication studies.

When writing, she writes with the direction of the Holy Spirit, in an effort to share with God's people all that He has for them.

In addition to teaching and writing, Dr. White-Elliott also serves as an evangelistic teacher. She is also the founder of International Women's Commission, a ministry that serves the needs of the entire person, by attending to healing the mind, body, soul, and spirit.

Dr. White-Elliott holds a Ph.D. in Education, a Master's in English Composition, and a Bachelor's in Education.

Dr. White-Elliott is also the founder of CLF Publishing, LLC. For your publishing needs, go online to www.clfpublishing.org.

OTHER BOOKS BY

THE AUTHOR

(All books can be purchased at

www.creativemindsbookstore)

From Despair, through Determination, to Victory!

A lot can happen during a span of 40 years. The life of Dr. Cassundra White-Elliott has been anything but uneventful. From a fun-loving childhood sprinkled with incidents of abuse to a tumultuous young adulthood to a stable, secure adult life, she has experienced a full life, with much more to come. Her story is inspiring and motivating.

If anyone lacks hope, reading Dr. White-Elliott's autobiography will propel him/her into an attitude of "Maybe I can." This attitude, if nurtured and developed, will grow into an attitude of "Yes, I can." Throughout her life, Cassundra has always held in her heart the belief that she could achieve anything that she had a made-up mind to embark upon. She was determined to achieve her heart's desires, doing what God has called her to do. She takes no credit for herself. All the glory goes to God, for He is her driving force. In Him, she lives, moves, and has her being.

Through the Storm

Through the Storm was duly inspired by the avaricious cloud of depression that decided to hover overhead of my daily existence in the latter part of 2007. Although I found it extremely difficult, I was once again compelled to not be defeated by just another snare that the enemy, the trickster, set for me. Once again, or more appropriately I should say *continuously*, he has exerted pernicious efforts to snatch the very life out of me by causing me to wallow in despair and to believe that I had been overcome by failure when in actuality and all reality, I was just experiencing a temporary setback. During those cloudy days, I had to remind myself daily that even though I was a target of the enemy, I am and will always be a child of the Most High god, Jehovah, who is my rock, my stability.

Unleashed Anger, Anger Unleashed

Preview

Introduction
What Is This Book All About?

As I prepared to embark upon the adventure of writing this book, I had to prepare myself to also be transparent. I have found that being transparent is required in order for healing to transpire, healing for all those that peruse the pages of this book and myself. And I may as well tell you that today, at the onset of this project, I have not been totally delivered from my condition of being an anger-filled person. However, I am definitely a work in progress. I have made strides with the assistance of my Lord and Savior, Jesus Christ, who is the head of my life. Without his love, guidance, and teachings, I would not be the woman of God I am today. I shudder to think where I could be instead and will therefore not entertain the thought.

Public Speaking in the Spiritual Arena

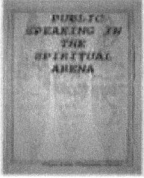

Preview

Chapter Two

How Communication Works

Purpose: This chapter will explain the six primary components of communication, identifying their purpose and how they work together.

The Source

In oral communication, the source of information is the speaker. In a church setting, the foundation of the message is God's word, but it is a speaker's interpretation of God's word that is delivered to the audience. As speakers vary, the information may vary but should have a similar essence because the foundational text is the same.

The Message

The message is the collective set of ideas that the speaker (the source) wants to deliver and/or illustrate to the audience. The message can be informative where the speaker informs the audience about a specific set of information. Or, the message may be persuasive in nature if the speaker wants to persuade the audience about conducting themselves in a specific manner, accepting God's commandments, or any number of things.

Where is Your Joppa?

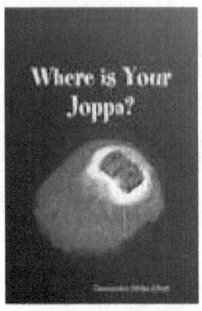

Introduction

Where is Your Joppa? was written for the express purpose of illustrating God's call for obedience in the lives of believers with respect to the individual call that He has on each of our lives. As you read throughout the various chapters, notice that the emphasis is placed on our persistent disobedience in answering God's call in a specific area of our lives. We have become a people who are similar to the Israelites when they found themselves in the middle of the wilderness, following their exodus from Egypt. Before God, they murmured and complained about their current life conditions and failed to be obedient to God's statutes delivered through His servant Moses. Their persistent disobedience caused them to lose the opportunity to see and enter the Promised Land. I ask you, "What has your disobedience cost you?" "Was your disobedience worth what it cost you?" "Do you think about the souls you could have ushered into the kingdom of God?" These are some of the questions that I pray will be answered through your reading of the book.

Mayhem in the Hamptons

Romero and Yolanda optimistically plan for the day that is going to change their lives from being single persons to a couple who is united in holy matrimony. They, along with their parents, close friends and family, fly over to the infamous Hamptons, where only the rich and famous vacation, to have their dream wedding at the five-star Hampton Suites located on a peninsula in the Hamptons. Little do they know that their perfect day will turn out to be less than perfect when their wedding planner Mariesha Coleman suddenly goes missing!

A time when the newlyweds' lives should be filled with joy and the creation of wonderful memories, they are stricken with grief as they desperately try to find clues to help solve Mariesha's disappearance.

Mayhem in the Hamptons is a tale that shares how the horrors of a woman's past can come back to haunt her in more than one way and the impact it can have on anyone who gets in the way.

Preacher's Daughter

Tinisha, the daughter of a preacher, is a twenty-six year old God-fearing young woman endeavoring to complete law school so that she can make her mark in the courtroom. Working in one of the late-night clubs in Hollywood to earn money to pay her own way through school, Tinisha soon learns that life doesn't always go as planned. Finding her strength in her faith, Tinisha constantly finds herself praying as she watches God move miraculously in her life.

Preacher's Son

Romero Turner is a private investigator with a promising future. As he continues to build his career, he is excited about the cases he undertakes. However, his father Pastor Theodore Turner has other plans for his son's life. In the midst of trying to save his client's husband from Sylvestor Domingo, a ruthless crime lord, Romero must try to salvage his relationship with his father. He must decide if ministry or life as a detective is in his future.

Lord, Teach Me to be a Blessing!

Lord, Teach Me to be a Blessing! will change a person's mentality from being centered around "me, myself, and I" to focusing on "others."

The world system teaches us that it is acceptable to place ourselves above others in an attempt to get ahead and even to survive. Herbert Spencer coined the phrase '*survival of the fittest*' after reading Charles Darwin's theory of evolution. This concept of surpassing and outdoing others is the world's philosophy.

However, the word of God does not subscribe to or promote this self-centered ideology, and therefore, neither should believers. We must hold fast to the truths outlined in Holy Scripture: "*Love thy neighbor as you love thyself*" (James 2:8) and "*It is more blessed to give than to receive*" (Acts 20:35). While holding God's truths to be self evident, we must demonstrate them to others, thereby showing them the way of the Lord of how to be a blessing to someone *rather* than looking to receive a blessing.

This is the very purpose of this book: to change the mentality of the world from being *self* centered to *other* centered.

After the Dust Settles

Throughout the journey of life, we all experience ups and downs and joys and pains. Most of us successfully find solutions to the situations/problems we encounter, but we often avoid dealing with the attached emotions. If we continue to ignore the emotions of pain, hurt, disappointment, anger, etc., we set ourselves up for destruction. Our families, our cultures, and our society tell us to be strong, to keep our chin up, and to grin and bear it. However, these methods of avoidance can lead us to strokes due to the undue amount of pressure we place on ourselves and/or mental illness from being unable to cope with the emotional baggage we have accumulated.

In *After the Dust Settles*, Dr. C. White-Elliott shares several situations that we all may encounter at one time or another in our lifetime and how to successfully navigate through them, so we can find ourselves emotionally healthy after the dust has settled and the situation has been rectified.

Begin reading today and experience a better tomorrow!